THE DESTINY CLUB

THE DESTINY CLUB

. . .

M. J. Walton

This book is dedicated to all of my gal pals, which includes my mom and the great ladies of The Foothills, and "Julie," my partner in crime (you know who you are).

ACKNOWLEDGEMENTS

SPECIAL THANKS: To Lynne Mahar, Suzy Walton and Christine Walton Cotner for helping me scout Strip locations, particularly the Linq; for driving around and around and around until we were dizzy. To Patricia Cichon for taking me to the Linq, driving around the Linq, walking the Linq Promenade with me, and helping me explore the Linq parking garage. To Areta Fleming for your keen editing eye and encouragement. To Judy Anderson for your invaluable editing help, especially with accents, for your support, and for being my unpaid publicity agent. To Barbara Berry for an early read and encouragement. To Lynne Maher, again, for your expert photo technical skills, and to Connie Rousseau for taking the photo. To my high school girlfriends, my college girlfriends, and my Las Vegas girlfriends for providing ideas and inspiration. And to my mom, Jane Pennington, who always believes in me. Without all of your support and help, this book would not have been possible.

Author's Note

Many of the Las Vegas locations mentioned in The Destiny Club are real:

Las Vegas Boulevard, also known as the Strip: Divided boulevard that runs north and south dividing the east and west sides of The Las Vegas Strip.

The Fremont Street Experience: A four-block pedestrian mall on Western Fremont Street in downtown Las Vegas. A 90-foot barrel vault canopy covers the four-block expanse on which a laser show is featured every hour after dark. The Fremont Street Experience also features multiple forms of entertainment: people dressed as characters, musicians, dancers, bands, performance artists, artisans who do quick landscapes using spray paint from cans, etc. Casinos, bars, restaurants and shops open onto the expanse for easy access. For the more adventuresome, there are also zip lines.

Henderson, Nevada: Separate, incorporated city adjoining Las Vegas on the far southeast side.

Summerlin: Upscale, master planned community located on far west side of Las Vegas. Summerlin was the name of Howard Hughes' grandmother.

Red Rock Canyon: Red Rock National Conservation Area, part of the Spring Mountains, is located on the far west side of Las Vegas near Summerlin. The Conservation area features beautiful red rock formations, frequented by hikers and rock climbers, and a picturesque thirteen-mile, one-way drive.

Downtown Summerlin: Commercial area on the west side of Las Vegas near Red Rock Casino which includes many upscale shops and restaurants.

Cleopatra's Barge: A classic Vegas lounge/bar located inside Caesars, loosely replicating a luxurious, Egyptian water craft that Cleopatra might have used; features live music.

Tivoli Village: Commercial area in Summerlin that includes upscale shops and boutiques, business offices, wine shops, restaurants, etc., plus dog-friendly areas. Buildings are in an old European-style architecture.

The Chandelier Bar: Located in the Cosmopolitan Casino Hotel on the Las Vegas Strip, the three-story Chandelier Bar is topped by a huge chandelier with beaded crystals cascading like curtains down the three tiers to the floor. Along with the spiral staircase, there is also a glass elevator for accessing the three levels. The Chandelier Bar menu features a number of specialty drinks.

The Linq and the Linq Promenade: The Linq (formerly the Imperial Palace) is a casino hotel located approximately midway on the east side of the Las Vegas Strip, across Las Vegas Boulevard from Caesars. The Linq Promenade is a picturesque, outdoor walk at the Linq that runs from Las Vegas Boulevard to the High Roller entrance. Along the Promenade are restaurants, bars, shops, etc.

The High Roller: Located on the Las Vegas Strip, behind The Linq Casino Hotel. The High Roller is the tallest rotating observation wheel (Ferris Wheel) in the world. Each of the twenty-eight glass pods can hold up to 40 people, and one rotation of the wheel takes 30 minutes to complete.

North Las Vegas: Separate, incorporated city adjoining Las Vegas on the far north side.

Las Vegas Trivia:

Las Vegas Climate: Although Las Vegas is located in the desert, it is also situated in a valley and is often referred to as "The Las Vegas Valley." The summers are hot ("but it's a dry heat"!) often rising into the one hundred teens. Winters can be quite chilly, sometimes dipping below freezing. Most years at least one snow flurry occurs, with occasional accumulation. Las Vegas has spring, summer, fall and winter, with a Monsoon season running through July and August, resulting in heavy rain and flash flooding.

 Driver License: Different states use different names for the license authorization to drive a motor vehicle. Some names: driver's license, driving license, driver license. In Nevada, it is driver license.

 Metro: Las Vegas Metropolitan Police Department.

 UNLV: University of Nevada Las Vegas

PROLOGUE

"Oh what a tangled web we weave,
When first we practise (sic) to deceive."

SIR WALTER SCOTT

WE NEVER DREAMED that this poetic quotation would ever apply to us. But Scott had surely nailed it when it came to the definition of *our* web of intrigue. Although in the beginning, there was no way we could have envisioned that our deceptive folly would lead us so deeply into a tangled web of serial murders that we would become suspects. Was one of us a serial killer?

CHAPTER 1

— • • • —

It started as a lark. Nothing more than a seemingly harmless diversion conjured by a group of bored, forty-something women looking for a little excitement in our rather ordinary lives. I can still vividly picture that afternoon in late February when the Destiny Club was conceived. The day started off dreary and chilly. Grey woolly clouds threatened any second to pour forth rain, prompting me to draw an anxious breath whenever I looked skyward. Even in Las Vegas the sun can't shine *every* day.

I was late getting to our luncheon, having had one of "those" mornings. I'm sure you know the kind I mean: when no matter what you do, everything seems to turn out wrong. In my haste, while pulling into the valet lane at Caesars, I clumsily overturned my large purse, spilling half the contents across the floor of the car and under the seat. I remember the startled look on the hapless parking valet's face when he met my car, wondering what he had done to cause me to curse like a sailor. I glanced at him in embarrassment just as I finished jamming the last of the spilled items back inside my purse. Trying to make amends for his mistaken belief that he was the cause of my wrath, I handed him a generous tip along with my car key.

I was meeting my old friends . . . well, we weren't exactly old . . . at least not yet; but we had been friends for more years than we cared to count. We had banded together in high school when none of us had been invited to join the in-group, and we proudly came to consider ourselves as the renegades. The nine of us had been a close-knit group since.

For a brief while after high school graduation, we had all held jobs in various Vegas casinos. A few of us had even enjoyed minor show business flings before venturing on our separate ways: some of us to other careers, some to attend college, and a few to get married. Eventually, we all ended up scattered to other parts of the country, except Julie, who remained in Las Vegas. However, throughout all of our years of being geographically apart, we had always kept in touch. In the past several years, by a fortunate twist of fate, we had all ended up once again living in Las Vegas. And recently, we had begun celebrating our reunion by meeting every other week at one of the higher end restaurants—often on the Strip—for long, leisurely lunches, accompanied by free-flowing wine.

Today we were meeting at Spago in Caesars. The others were already at the table when I joined them, some by now into their second glass of wine.

"Hi, Jayne, we're glad you made it! We were beginning to worry," said Julie, handing me a glass of pinot noir.

"We've been discussing the miserable weather. This is such a dismal time of year, don't you think?" remarked Deena.

As a matter of fact I did; mostly because I was still having difficulty trying to adjust to the unexpected loss of my husband, Marc, a little over a year ago. One morning he had left the house as usual for work, but never came home. He had been found shortly before noon slumped over his desk. The autopsy found that he had died suddenly from an aortic aneurysm. I was still filled with a mixture of anguish and anger that—had we known—a simple ultrasound could have most likely saved his life. I had been trying to cope with my anger and my aloneness by throwing myself into trying to jump-start a career in fiction writing. So far, I hadn't had much luck, which left me feeling pretty much a failure in addition to my loneliness. It also didn't help matters that I had "celebrated" my forty-sixth birthday several weeks ago. I found the thought of being less than four years away from the milestone of fifty to be particularly depressing.

I knew my friends were concerned about the way I would often retreat into my shell and become reclusive. I forced a smile as I said, "You've got that right, Deena. It will take some kind of a miracle to pep things up in my life."

"I hear you loud and clear," agreed Nikki, saluting with her half-empty glass of chardonnay.

Actually, we had all been very fortunate, and we should have been more appreciative of our blessings . . . but maybe that's just human nature. We had all married well (some of us two, three—even four times "well"). Those of us who had become parents had great kids, and one of us, Kayla, had already become a "young" grandmother. Only two of us were presently single: I was the token widow, and Cassandra had gone through an amicable, mutually-agreed-upon divorce six months ago.

Perhaps it was just the fact that in our youth we had all envisioned ourselves as someday being deeply absorbed in exhilarating, successful careers and rewarding marriages. Now that children had grown up and husbands were busy furthering their careers, frequently requiring them to be away, the time often seemed to drag. Memories of our early ambitions and idealistic aspirations seemed to have transmuted into haunting reminders of our unfulfilled dreams. We missed the thrill of looking forward to new adventures. Our youthful anticipations of stimulating challenges lying ahead had degenerated into merely more years of sameness: each day a duplicate of the one previously passed, with each adding a greater accumulation of wrinkles, sags (damned gravity!), and cellulite.

"C'mon, let's not get started on a downer before we even order lunch," pleaded Julie. "It's just the icky weather that's making us feel this way. When spring comes, everything will seem different. You'll see, we just need—"

"Oh, Julie, You're always such a damned optimist about everything!" Nikki interrupted. "It's not just the weather. We're all growing older, and we need something exciting to perk up our lives. What do we do? We shop, go out to dinner once or twice a week, attend an occasional movie or show, spend time with our kids, when they have time for us, and anticipate our physical and mental declines. Our evening socializations mostly consist of attending dull business functions with our husbands, where we associate with people we scarcely know, and probably don't even care to know! What do we ever do that's *really* fun, or exciting, or important—other than these lunches every two weeks?"

Nikki's outburst was met with a resounding silence. I guess we had been abruptly thrust into an unpleasant realization. Her assessment had been brutally accurate, causing us to face head-on something that had previously only been uncomfortably flittering in the back of our minds.

"I don't know about the rest of you, but I never realized my life could be this boring," stated Tiffani, as she scanned the menu. "But then I feel so guilty even thinking such thoughts—let alone voicing them aloud—when I look at other people's lives and know how much I have to be thankful for."

"I wish sometimes that I could be someone else for a while . . . someone totally different from the way I am," Deena confessed sheepishly, "just for the hell of it!"

All but Kayla spontaneously nodded in agreement.

"Wouldn't that be fun?" exclaimed Nikki.

"That does sound like it would be a very interesting and amusing experience," concurred Julie.

"Oh, wouldn't it though," affirmed Tiffani. "Sometimes I almost feel like I'm one of the 'Stepford Wives.'"

"Hey, we must be regressing! This is starting to sound like one of the wacky kind of things we used to talk about when we were in high school," Cassandra said, laughing.

"You know, sometimes when I would read about those people with the split personalities—especially those mousy women whose other personalities would manifest as strippers or hookers, or some other type of outrageous behavior, I always secretly envied them," Amber confided, almost in a whisper. "Sometimes I used to almost wish that I would develop one of those other personalities. Then I would have no guilt feelings over what I would do when I was that other person, because I would have no control over it. I would have an excuse for wild behavior. Maybe that's why I drink more than I should once in a while. I'm searching for that freedom to be myself."

"Amber, I've felt that very same way," disclosed Chloe. "But I never realized anyone else had, too."

One member of our group continued to remain conspicuously quiet.

"Kayla," I said, "I notice you're the only one who hasn't voiced a comment. I guess you and Larry are still on your cloud-nine honeymoon?"

Kayla had been married less than a year to her high school sweetheart. They had reconnected at our last high school reunion after a twenty-five-year loss of contact. It had been rekindled love at first sight the second time around, and they had decided that they had been meant for each other after all.

"Yeah, I'm happy to admit—as well as feeling a little guilty after what the rest of you have acknowledged—that Larry and I are still deliriously enamored with each other. And we're still enjoying trying to make up for all of those lost years! But as you well know, from my past mistakes I can certainly relate to what you all are saying. I, too, have been there, before Larry and I got our second chance to be together."

"Well, we all understand, and we are happy for you . . . even if we are just a wee bit envious," I answered with a grin.

The rest nodded in unison, then raised their glasses in a spontaneous chorus of cheers.

Although our luncheons had never taken such a seriously honest turn during the eight months we had been meeting, we all felt something of profound importance was happening: something that we all needed to have happen, and something that could only have occurred within our close little group—never with anyone else.

When we saw the waiter approaching our table, we paused in our digression for him to take our lunch orders. When he returned with two more bottles of wine, we scarcely noticed, as we were still mired in our abstracted ponderings of this unexpected—yet not unwelcome—epiphany that seemed to be taking place. Funny what rotten weather and a little wine can provoke.

By now my fiction-writer's imagination was in full rev mode, giving way to a brainstorm! When I could no longer contain my excitement, I stood and tapped on my wine glass with my spoon to get everyone's attention. "You know, maybe the fantasy of becoming another person isn't as farfetched as you all might think. Oh, I don't mean that we could literally flip out and develop a personality disorder like 'Sybil' or 'Eve.' And I'm not suggesting identity theft—at least not in the literal sense of ripping someone off. But it might be possible for us to create a woman we could take turns being . . . sort of an evil twin/alter ego that would allow us the freedom to do things we might not ordinarily have the nerve to do."

My enthusiasm was apparently contagious, because everyone was staring at me with an expression of hopeful interest mingled with doubt.

"Let me think on it a bit longer. . . ."

The waiter brought our food, and even the epicurean Spago cuisine was unable to vie for the attention my idea was generating. I could feel the undercurrent of electricity. I thoughtfully sliced off a piece of my roasted, herbed chicken breast as my mind worked on organizing my inspiration.

By the time we were ready for dessert (we definitely felt we deserved something decadently rich to celebrate this possible birthing of our conglomerate alter ego), I had my idea fairly well formulated. Now all that was left was to fill in the details.

As we divided the desserts among us—scrumptious concoctions of chocolate and luscious creations of liqueurs, nuts and gobs of whipped cream—I could feel my adrenalin pumping. I hadn't felt so alive since . . . well, certainly not since before I had lost Marc.

I savored a mouthful of first the chocolate, then the liqueur flavors, before elaborating on my idea.

"OK, what I have come up with is this: we create a woman . . . with a complete identity, as different from all of us as we can make her. We'll give her a name, get her a driver license, an address, etc. We'll even open a checking account in her name and get her a debit card, which hopefully won't be too difficult to do. Maybe we'll even get her a credit card later on once we get her identity established. I think our first step though is to agree on a name for her . . . what do you think of Destiny as her first name? I think it's rather appropriate, myself. But if any of you have another preference, we can take a vote."

I had their full attention as the rich desserts—now all but forgotten—melted on our plates, and they all murmured their approval.

"But what will we do with this woman—Destiny—after we create her?" asked Nikki, usually the most pragmatic member of our group.

"It's simple! We'll make her as mysterious and beguiling as possible. Then we'll take turns being her!"

"But we're all different heights and weights and colorings. I don't see how it could possibly work," Nikki persisted.

"I realize that, Nikki," I explained. "We will wear a wig, after deciding what shade and style. I favor long, curly, auburn hair—the way Reba McEntire wore hers before she had it cut shorter—as none of us wear our hair that way. And we will dress as glamorously and provocatively as we desire and dare. We all wear contact lenses, so we'll each just get an extra pair in whatever color we decide Destiny's eyes should be. I suggest deep blue. As a matter of fact, how often have any of us had our driver licenses checked lately? And when a license is checked, how often has the height and weight been scrutinized? Most often when a license is checked, it's while we're sitting; therefore height and weight are, for the most part, inconsequential. The birth date and license expiration date are probably the items most often checked. Second to that are probably the hair and eye color, to see if they match. The photo is usually only given a cursory glance to see if it is a reasonable likeness, and if it is, that's all that matters. It's not like any of us still get carded when we order a drink." I paused, as this remark elicited a few chuckles. "And certainly none of us will be using Destiny's ID to try to board an airplane," I added with a grin.

"We'll choose a median height and weight—the taller ones of us will wear lower-heeled shoes when we are Destiny, and the shorter ones will wear higher heels. Maybe five feet five inches tall and one hundred twenty pounds; I'll think more about that before making a final decision. We can all take turns being Destiny for a night whenever we want. Since there will only be one Destiny at any given time, there would never be an opportunity for someone to compare one Destiny against another. Oh, I know it will work. And just think, as Destiny, we'll have the chance to act out our most secret, wildest fantasies . . . whatever they may be!"

"Well, I still have my doubts. It sounds like it would be much too complicated," responded Nikki, shaking her head.

"Oh, I bet we can do it!" declared Deena.

"I think it sounds like a fantastically fun idea, and I can hardly wait for my turn. I wonder how I would look with long, auburn hair," said Cassandra, as she got out her compact and studied her face in the mirror.

"I think it sounds like fun, too!" agreed Julie. "Count me in, but I'm going to leave working out all the final details to you, Jayne."

"OK, that's fine . . . how about the rest of you? Who else wants to try it?"

"It's so bad, it's good," said Deena, grinning. You can definitely count me in!"

"Me, too," chimed in Chloe.

"And me," said Amber.

"Well, since the rest of you want to do it, then I'll go along with it," conceded Nikki. "However, I still have my doubts as to how we can pull it off."

"I think it would be a blast!" said Tiffani.

"I don't know if they use the word 'blast' anymore, Tiffani," chided Nikki.

"Well then, what word do they use?"

"I'm not sure, but I don't think it's 'blast.'"

"Well, whatever! Who cares what the word is, anyway!"

I looked around the table; everyone seemed enthusiastic except Kayla, our newly-wed. "What about you, Kayla? Do you want to be included if I can figure out how we can do it?"

She gave an exaggerated sigh, then smiled. "Well, although I doubt I will have much need to use it, if everyone else wants to try it, you can add me to the list. It may turn out to be fun at that."

"Good!" I said smiling, as ideas whirled in my mind. The more I thought about it, the more impassioned I became! "OK, we'll need a last name for our new 'self.' How about Sumner, the last name of my favorite singer? I think Destiny Sumner sounds like a good name."

"No, we should get to vote on that," said Julie. "I suggest Presley, the last name of MY favorite singer. You know how much I love the old, fifties rock. And, after all, Elvis isn't just 'The King'! He is 'The King' of Las Vegas!"

"Yeah, Presley is my favorite name, too!" agreed Amber. It's only fitting, being that we live in Las Vegas. Besides, who in the heck is the singer with the last name of Sumner? He's probably somebody no one's ever heard of. . . . Now, who all are in favor of Presley?"

"Wait a minute!" I interjected. "Doesn't Destiny Presley sound kind of fake? Think about it . . . okay, I know some of you want Destiny to have one of Elvis' names. But I suggest using his middle name: Aaron. Don't you think Destiny Aaron sounds better than Destiny Presley? And you would still be giving Elvis the honor of using one of his names. But we need to vote to be fair, and I still haven't given up on my choice of Sumner—which, by the way, is Sting's real last name. Does anyone else have another name to be considered? No? Okay, then we'll vote. All in favor of Sumner, raise your hands . . . well, don't everyone move at once! Thanks, Kayla. That's two votes for Sumner. Now, how many are in favor of Presley? No one? How about Aaron? Seven votes for Aaron. I guess that does it then: Destiny Aaron it is. I'll work on getting all the particulars fine-tuned. I should have most of them worked out in a couple of weeks. Is it OK with everyone if I decide on the hair, eyes, height and weight details? Since I'll need a little time to work this out, shall we make it three weeks instead of our usual two weeks before we meet again for lunch? Would Maggiano's at the Fashion Show Mall suit everybody?"

Everyone eagerly answered in the affirmative to both my questions.

We took our time leaving, dividing into smaller groups of twos and threes, some staying in the Forum area to do some shopping, with others striking out in different directions. We always made sure that the effects of whatever we had to drink had worn off before driving home. I was just anxious to go home so I could get busy figuring out how we could pull this off.

When I retrieved my car, from a different valet this time, I was chuckling. He gave me an odd look, and I'm sure he was probably thinking that I had partaken in too much of the grape—or was maybe high on God knows what else! But my second glass of wine I had finished over an hour ago was not the reason for my buoyant mood. It was the outlandish mental image of me in a long-haired, curly auburn wig and vampy clothes! The sky still looked ominous as I drove home. But I couldn't have cared less. My mind was occupied with giving Destiny Aaron life!

CHAPTER 2

———————— • • • ————————

EVEN THOUGH IT had been fourteen months since I had lost Marc, I was still unable to completely extricate myself from the grieving process. Just when I would seem to be making my way back to a semblance of normalcy, I would suffer the sudden regression of finding myself again stuck in the grieving loop: to once more be entrenched in the all too familiar pit of self-pity, which I loathed! Then I would have to start my trek back to some kind of normalcy all over again. I had read there is no set time limit for grieving. And that the five stages of grief aren't necessarily in sequence or experienced only one at a time. I was finding both of these to be true.

But today, when I arrived home from the luncheon at Caesars, to my amazement I realized that my thoughts weren't focused on my loneliness. That I was actually experiencing the beginning sensation of a type of spiritual renewal; something I had not felt since losing Marc. Maybe having to figure out how to give Destiny life was just what I needed: a project that would be so demanding of my time and focus that it would leave no time for preoccupation with grief and sadness.

Hally, my sweet, little calico, met me at the door. Even she could sense my change in mood. She and Marc had been best buddies. I knew that she also missed him and was grieving his loss in her own way. She used to lie for hours, devotedly nestled against his shoulder while he watched television. Sometimes she would now look at me with such a sorrowful, questioning expression in her eyes, as if asking me why he wasn't with us.

I scooped her up and carried her to Marc's favorite chair. Although she never nestled against my shoulder, she enjoyed snuggling in my lap. I sat down, and once we had both made ourselves comfortable, we sat together for hours in relative mutual contentment: Hally napping and purring as I stroked her, and I lost in my thoughts of how to pull off inventing Destiny.

Unfortunately, I had been so caught up in the initial excitement of giving Destiny life, that in my zeal, I hadn't paused long enough to fully consider what all would be involved. I tended to do that: pounce upon an idea with utter exuberance, only to discover later that I should have taken the time to fully process all of the aspects.

And so it was with Destiny. Perplexed, I shook my head, wondering if I was up to the challenge. Perhaps Destiny was one of those proverbial blessings in disguise, I hoped, that would be so demanding of my focus, concentration, and time it would end up being just what the doctor ordered.

One of my best avenues for processing ideas was being physically active, and swimming in my pool was my favorite form of activity for processing. Unfortunately the cold, gloomy February weather prohibited swimming. Therefore, after my quiet time of meditation with Hally, I walked on my treadmill, instead, mulling over various ideas. When I finished my workout, I sat down at my computer and began making a list of all of the various details to be taken care of, stopping only to drink several cups of tea and eat a snack of microwave popcorn. Not the kind of microwave popcorn that comes in a bag containing orange-colored chemicals masquerading as butter; but rather corn kernels that I popped in a glass bowl with *real* melted butter.

I had become so engrossed in my project that before I realized it, the hours had flown by, and it was after 11:00 p.m.: time for bed. Since losing Marc, I had come to dread bedtime and usually had difficulty falling asleep. Although Hally helped somewhat to fill the void, snuggling next to me in bed, I missed being able to fall asleep cuddled next to Marc, his arms around me, holding me.

Most nights when I went to bed I watched old black and white mystery movies on the Turner Classic Movie channel to help me fall asleep. I had found this to be the most effective non-pharmaceutical sleep aid in helping me to wind down and relax so I could drift off to dreamland. I kept my DVR filled with Film Noir, feeling secure that if I fell asleep before the end of a movie, I could always watch it again and never actually miss an ending.

Tonight it was *Conflict*, starring Humphrey Bogart. Even with my Film Noir sleep aid, I usually woke up several times during the night. However, for the first time in months, I slept soundly through the night, logging in a good seven-and-a-half hours.

When I woke up, I picked up the list on my nightstand that I had written on my computer and printed out last night. I started going over it again. Unfortunately, since the horrific 9/11 tragedy, it had become very difficult, if not virtually impossible, to do anything legal without a "valid" picture ID; which is, in turn, an equally difficult item to obtain. Criminals seem to be able to easily establish new identities—or steal someone else's identity. However, for honest people like us, it's damned hard to do! Oh, maybe we weren't being totally honest, but we certainly weren't intending to establish a fake ID in order to commit any kind of criminal acts.

I recognized that obtaining an ID for Destiny was definitely going to take some doing on my part, and I began to have doubts: *had I blithely undertaken something that was beyond my capabilities?* Well, I had to start someplace, I resolved. First things first: her looks. So I got out of bed, got dressed, and went shopping!

It didn't take long for me to find the perfect Reba-style wig, which, even if I do say so myself, looked very becoming on me. I was also able to decide on the perfect color of contact lenses: an unusual, deep blue violet color, which I already had. I shopped for clothes, the type that I had never been gutsy enough to wear, and enjoyed trying on the outrageous styles. What fun I was having!

The next day, after donning the wig, the deep blue contact lenses, and a newly- purchased outfit in black leather that I thought particularly befitting Destiny's persona, it was time to get her a Nevada driver license. That was when the Destiny project turned out to no longer be fun.

Filled with naïve confidence, I went to the nearest DMV. After checking in, I took a number, and after nearly a two-hour wait (you know how long those lines are at the DMV), my number finally came up. And, to my good fortune—or so I thought—my interviewer turned out to be a man. I fancied I could play on his sympathy with a well-rehearsed hard luck story, embellished with a mixture of winsome eye batting and woeful pleading.

I would have guessed him to be in his late forties to early fifties. He was rather a plain-looking man, clean shaven, with receding dark blond hair. His hazel eyes peered at me over his bifocals, which he wore low on his nose, giving an owlish appearance that I found rather comical. I had to fight to keep from smiling. I noticed he was wearing some kind of school ring on his right hand, but was not wearing a wedding band. He also had on a wrist watch, which possibly indicated he was not a cell phone techie. (Most cell phone techies that I knew did not wear a wrist watch.) Maybe this meant that he was an old fashioned guy with a big heart, I hoped!

I took a deep breath and began my wistful tale with bravado. "You see, sir, I recently moved here from Florida, and I lost all of my identification when my purse was stolen shortly after my arrival. It's just awful! I can't even find a job. No one will hire me without an ID. Therefore I desperately need a driver license."

I now wished I wasn't wearing such an outlandish outfit; however it had been necessary for Destiny's photo on the license. Too late, I realized that my attire was not the wisest clothing choice for evoking sympathy. *Why hadn't I had the forethought to bring along a modest sweater to wear over my Destiny outfit until picture-taking time?* I could feel my bravado running out with a fast swoosh.

"Well, ma'am, I'll surely see what I can do to help you out," the clerk said, breaking into a toothy grin, which I wasn't sure was a come-on grin, or merely a friendly grin. In my new persona, my judgment was off kilter. Plus, I had been out of "the game" too long. I did note that he had nice, even, teeth.

"What I can do," he continued ingratiatingly, "is contact the Florida DMV and try to obtain a copy of your license from there. If I can do that, then it's a simple matter to issue you a new Nevada license."

I was so taken aback, all I could do was utter "Oh!" *I hadn't thought of that possibility, and I certainly couldn't let him contact Florida for a license that had, of course, never existed!*

I felt like my mind was grappling, trying to find a way out of this surprising muddle I had created. I should have been more prepared for the unexpected.

I coughed, stalling for time, and finally confessed awkwardly: "I never had a Florida license; I never needed one. But now that I'm in Nevada, I do need a license."

"Ma'am, what, may I ask, did you use for ID when you lived in Florida?"

Now that question really did frazzle me! I certainly hadn't done proper advance planning for this. I had to come up with something plausible, and fast! My heart rate began to quicken as I started to feel like I was losing control of the situation; therefore it did not take much of an effort for tears to well in my eyes.

"Well, you see, I haven't needed an ID for a number of years," I said, the tears now sliding down my face—partly from frustration, and partly from despair. I was beginning to fear that obtaining a license in Destiny's name might turn out to be an impossibility. *But that would be unacceptable! I would have to find a way!*

I took a deep breath, squared my shoulders, and tried to calm myself as I began to invent my story. "When I lived in Florida, I was in a long-term relationship, and I was very well taken care of financially. I didn't need to work or drive. But then," I said in a husky voice that I didn't have to fake. "But then . . . my boyfriend suddenly found someone else. And he dumped me! Oh, it's still so painful to talk about." I began to sob. "I just don't know what I'm going to do. I don't have much work experience, and I have to find some kind of a job here in Vegas in order to support myself. But, as I told you, I can't do that without some form of ID. I can't even rent an apartment or open a bank account without an ID. I am presently having to stay at one of the women's shelters."

Now *he* was the one who was thrown off kilter, obviously by my story and possibly by my tears. I experienced a welcome surge of relief; maybe I was finally on a roll, the invented story coming easily. *Good job, Jayne, I thought, congratulating myself on my ingenuity!*

He bent down and opened one of his lower desk drawers, grabbed an open box of Kleenex and pushed it toward me.

I pulled out some tissues and dried my eyes. Then I gazed at him with what I hoped was one of the most soulfully sad expressions he had ever seen. "Please help me," I pleaded, batting my eyelashes for good measure.

He sighed, and he really did look sympathetic as he explained, "I'm really very sorry, but there is nothing I can do right now to help you get a license. You need some type of valid ID in order to get a license . . . like a copy of your birth certificate."

He gave the impression he was ready to wind things up with me so he could move on to the next number. But I wasn't ready for that. My mind seemed to be clicking along now, my writer's imagination finally having kicked in!

"I'm afraid that would be impossible. I've never had a birth certificate. You see, I was a foundling left on the steps of an orphanage when

I was an infant. They could never find out who my parents were." I knew I was really reaching with that explanation, but it was the first thing I could come up with on the spur of the moment. His eyes widened in disbelief. I doubted if he had ever run across anyone quite like me before in his professional capacity. He was probably the type who fancied himself the ultimate problem solver.

He frowned, drumming his fingers on the desk for several seconds before suggesting, "I guess then you need to write to the orphanage for help. They should be able to help you find some kind of documentation—maybe a baptismal certificate? Perhaps someone at the women's shelter where you're staying could help you do that. Don't they have a social worker?"

I knew I was totally reaching out of bounds now, as I answered: "Unfortunately, the orphanage is no longer there. It was closed and razed sixteen years ago."

I fixed my eyes steadily on his with my continued soulful look. He stared back at me with a look of such incredulity, I thought he probably believed I was either the most miserably unlucky person alive, or that I had just told him the biggest whopper imaginable. He seemed so befuddled that I nearly felt sorry for him.

Finally he looked away and sighed as he stood up, indicating that the interview was over. He cleared his throat, then licked his lips before saying: "I'm sorry. I hope someone at the shelter where you are staying can help you find the records you need. Good luck to you."

"Well, thank you for your time, anyway," I murmured. I slowly rose to my feet, pausing briefly to smooth down my mini skirt before turning to leave. I thought I could feel his eyes on my back, watching me as I walked away, and I couldn't help swinging my hips a little; I stopped for an instant to turn around to see if my suspicions were correct. They were!

But now I had to try to find a way to get a fake license. Only I wasn't sure where or how to go about it. I needed to bounce this problem off someone else. When I got to my car, I called Julie on my cell. Several days later, after we had discussed the various options and given the matter much thought, the two of us decided that the most likely opportunity would be found on Fremont Street, where the performance artists performed their *art*—among other things.

I thought it best that I try it alone. I didn't want to attract any more attention than necessary to my quest, and if Julie was with me, someone might mistake us for undercover cops. As it turned out, I ended up having to cruise Fremont Street three nights in a row, plus waiting two more nights, before finally hitting pay dirt.

I decided not to dress as Destiny, as well as to disguise my usual look. I had a feeling that it would be best for me not to be associated with our future Destiny persona. The first night, hoping to give the impression of being a tourist, I wore jeans, a T-shirt from the Beatles *Love* Cirque show, and a black leather, moto-style jacket. I covered my mid-back length blonde hair with a dark brown wig in a short style.

I valet parked at the Golden Nugget, then made my way through the casino to an exit onto Fremont Street. Outside, the air was chilly, and I soon grew uncomfortable walking up and down the expanse, sizing up prospects. Although in my opinion several looked to be promising, to my dismay, I found that I was more of a wimp than I realized. I began to wonder if I had the necessary chutzpah to fulfill my mission. I finally psyched myself into action and sidled up to a well-built man painted entirely in metallic silver, clad only in a bright green thong decorated with green leaves. I wasn't sure how to begin the conversation, so I gave him what I hoped was an alluring grin. "Hi," I ventured somewhat hesitantly. I wasn't used to talking to strange men, and believe me, this one, although probably attractive to some, perfectly fitted the definition of strange!

"I'm new to the area," I continued. I realized he was hustling money by having his picture taken with tourists. So I had my picture taken with him in return for giving him what I thought to be a more than adequate tip. I hoped this would entitle me to a little in-depth conversation.

I hung around until the crowd had slacked off a bit, then gave him my alluring grin again (at least I hoped it was alluring!), and asked: "Would you like to have a drink with me, my treat?"

"Look, lady, I don't mean to be rude, but I'm working. Besides that, I'm gay."

I wasn't sure how to respond. Maybe it would be best to simply be honest.

"I'm really not trying to come on to you. I just need to find someone who can help me get a Nevada driver license for ID. It's very important."

"Lady, what you're asking for is against the law. Just because I work on Fremont Street doesn't mean that I'm into any kind of shady deals. And even if I was, how do I know that you're not a cop?"

I could feel my face turning red from the heat of embarrassment. I had really blown this attempt! "Sorry," I muttered as I walked away, trying to size up other prospects. I decided from now on I would need to be more careful.

I continued my perusing until it was nearly Midnight, and eventually decided to approach an enchantingly attractive woman garbed as a Disney Snow White. She had flawless, fair skin, and thick, glossy dark hair piled on top of her head. *A wig, I wondered?* She wore a black lace-up bustier, and a stiff, white, fan-shaped collar at the back of her neck. Her ankle-length skirt was magenta and mauve striped, with gold metallic threads running through the taffeta-type fabric. And, although her costume was beautiful, her breasts—the perfect size and shape— were totally exposed except for shiny gold, apple-shaped pasties barely covering her nipples. I couldn't help wondering how the folks at Disney would feel about that.

I hoped that maybe I could appeal to her, woman to woman. When she had a lull, I walked up to her and smiled. "Your costume is lovely," I said with genuine sincerity.

"Thank you," she answered, giving me a smile in return. "I designed and made it myself."

"Wow! You are very talented," I said, and meant it.

"Yeah, it's too bad I have to expose my tits, but that's what gives me the largest tips."

She sighed, then continued, as if she felt the need to defend herself. "Actually, I studied costume design in California. After I moved here I worked as a costume designer for one of the Strip shows until it closed and I was laid off. I have a three-year-old daughter to support, and until I can find another designing gig, this is the best money I've found. It's amazing what tourists will pay to have their picture taken with me, especially after they've had a few drinks."

This gave me the perfect opening. "I'm new in town, and I'd love to treat you to a drink if you can take a break."

She gave a hasty glance in both directions at the thinning crowd of revelers. "Sure, why not? Maybe a quick one."

She shrugged into a heavy, red knitted sweater and pulled it tightly across her bare bosom. With her leading the way, we strolled across to one of the outdoor street bars and found a place to sit. After we had ordered our drinks—a glass of cabernet for me and an imported beer for her, she began to eye me dubiously.

"Okay, I'm curious. What exactly is it that you want? I don't think you invited me for a drink solely out of the goodness of your heart. Are you also a performance artist, looking to get in on the action? Or are you looking for something else? If you're looking for a sexual tryst, I'm straight, and I don't turn tricks or do group sex."

Initially her candidness took me by surprise. But then, again, it would be only natural for her to suspect me of having an ulterior motive.

"I *am* looking for something, but not for a gig . . . or sex! I'm looking for a referral to someone who can provide me with a fake Nevada driver license."

Her eyes filled with anger as she shook her head. "Look, just because I work on Fremont Street doesn't mean I'm privy to information like that. I don't even socialize with the rest of the artists. All I'm doing is trying to make a living here to take care of the needs of my little girl and myself. This is only temporary until I can find a more substantial means of support."

By now her eyes were blazing, and I was genuinely sorry that she felt I had insulted her. I knew I quickly needed to gain her sympathy if I was to get anywhere with her. I looked ruefully down into my glass. "I'm really sorry if I offended you. That was certainly not my intention. I need help, and I don't know where to turn." Then I commenced to give her an abbreviated version of the same hard luck fabrication I had related to the DMV clerk, even managing to squeeze out a few tears.

Her eyes remained impassive during my narration, and when I finished, she frowned, but made no comment. She continued to sip her beer as she contemplated my story. My stomach was doing flip-flops while I waited for her to say something. Finally her face softened, indicating she had decided to buy it.

"Gee, that's rough. Some men are just no good! I've certainly met my share of those!"

I nodded in commiseration.

She remained deep in thought while she finished drinking her beer, then rose from her seat and looked up and down the street. "I don't know of anyone personally, but if you can find Jade, the belly dancer," she said, lowering her voice, "I think she would probably be able to put you in touch with someone to get you what you need. But don't tell her I sent you! Just go up to her and offer to buy her to a drink, the way you did me, and then tell her what you need and why. I don't see her now—she may have already gone home. She gets some of the biggest tips of any of us on Fremont Street. She doesn't work every night—she doesn't have to."

She gave me a tired smile. "I need to get home to my daughter now. It's almost time for her sitter to leave. Good luck to you. I hope you can find what you need. Maybe we'll run into each other again sometime."

"Thanks for your help. I hope things will turn around for you and you will be able to find another costume designing job very soon. And yes, I hope we will meet again," I said, sincerely meaning my good wishes for her. Tonight I had begun to view the Fremont Street performance artists in a totally different way.

The following night I visited Fremont Street, with my same wig, jeans and jacket as the night before, but this time with a different T-shirt. I walked up and down the blocks looking for Jade, with no avail. But on the third night, my labors were rewarded.

I had done my usual stroll up and down the street, searching, stopping only once to rest my feet and have a glass of wine before continuing. I was about to give up when I finally spotted her. Although she must have just begun her dance, she already had a large gathering around her, all of whom seemed very anxious to reward her undulating body by slipping bills under the straps of her bra or in the side of her belt. I have to admit, she was spectacular!

Her slender, lithe body was executing undulations the likes of which I had never seen before, or even imagined possible. She reminded me of a graceful snake. Her skin was the color of light copper, and her silky hair—the color of dark chocolate streaked with caramel highlights—fell nearly to her waist. Her costume consisted of an ornately beaded bra in coral with a matching coral beaded belt. Multiple strands of gold coins hung from the bottom edge of each. Her skirt consisted of volumes of scarlet chiffon that swirled around her as she twirled.

She had miniature brass cymbals affixed to the thumb and middle finger of each hand. When she hit them together, they sounded like the delicate tinkling of tiny bells. In addition to the finger cymbals, her dancing was accompanied by exotic, Middle Eastern music playing from a small Bose CD player, and a man dressed in a sultan's costume playing an unusual looking drum. Both the Bose and the drummer were sitting on the edge of a small rug of Persian design. Next to the drummer, a small, deep wicker basket without a lid had been placed, presumably for tips, since it contained a number of bills. In the middle of the rug sat another, slightly larger, wicker basket with a lid covering the top. I, along with the rest of the large crowd watching her, was entranced. She used every part of her body in her dance, including her hair.

Partway through her dance her music slowed, and she moved to the center of the rug where she undulated to her knees in front of the basket. When she lifted the basket's lid, a small, round head appeared: the head of a snake! She gently lifted the snake into the air, holding it in front of her for a few seconds before draping it across her head and down onto her shoulders. The snake was about five feet in length and well trained. It began to slither down her left shoulder and across her abdomen, perfectly in sync with her undulations. It was really quite mesmerizing!

After about ten minutes, she finished with a flourish, giving a sweeping bow. I could see bills in denominations of twenties and up. Not only were they peeking out from her bra and belt, but the open tip basket sitting beside her Bose player was nearly overflowing.

I wasn't sure how to get her attention, other than with money. I pulled a fifty dollar bill from my purse, and I made sure she was watching as I dropped it in the tip basket while nodding my head, hoping to indicate my wanting to talk to her. She nodded back.

As the crowd began to move away, I stood next to her tip basket, waiting for her as she approached. She walked as gracefully as she danced.

"Did you want something?" She asked, with the slight trace of an accent.

I nodded in the affirmative. She was still holding her snake, and I felt my pulse quicken as she moved closer to me. I had always been afraid of snakes, and to be so unexpectedly close to one, I could feel the adrenalin rush beginning the flight or fight surge. Even though I tried to stifle my fear, she couldn't help noticing my unease, which she seemed to find amusing.

She laughed as she said: "Oh, this is Brian. You don't need to be afraid of him. He's really quite harmless." And she actually kissed him on top of his head while placing him back inside his basket.

Before attempting to speak, I swallowed and cleared my throat, trying to compose my thoughts. Besides being in awe of her talent, I was still somewhat shaken from being so close to Brian. I didn't want to screw up my request of her by asking in the wrong way.

"You are an amazing artist," I said, then stopped, unsure of how to segue into the information I needed from her.

She did a quick, little half bow as she said, "Thank you." Then she gazed at me quizzically, her smoky, obsidian eyes seeming to penetrate into mine. "And. . . ."

"Can I buy you a drink?" I blurted, trying to make the situation less awkward, but probably only making it more so.

"Why? Why do you want to buy me a drink? If you're hitting on me, you need to know up front before you waste your time that I'm straight. I like men."

I could feel the flush of embarrassment coloring my cheeks. That was three times now that my motives had been mistaken for something of a sexual nature. "Oh, no," I stammered. "It's nothing like that. But I would like to talk with you."

During our brief verbal exchange she had been busily plucking the tucked bills from her costume and stuffing them in her tip basket. I stood, watching her, waiting until she finished for her reply. Then she shrugged. "Okay. I need a little rest break, and a drink would be nice."

She threw a velvet cape over her shoulders, which I noticed matched the scarlet color of the chiffon in her skirt; she nodded to her drummer while giving him some kind of a hand signal. "Follow me," she said, as she picked up her tip basket and began threading her way through the frolicking throng of tourists and locals to a particular sidewalk bar. Thankfully, it was a different bar from where I had treated Snow White to a drink two nights ago; I didn't want anyone remembering me as a frequent customer.

After we were comfortably seated, we ordered our drinks—a cabernet again for me, and for her, something I had never heard of called raki.

Getting straight to the point she again fixed her eyes on mine as she said, "I'm feeling vibes that you want something from me."

I was a bit surprised by her bluntness; but in a way I was also grateful that she had made the opening.

"Well, as a matter of fact I do. I am hoping you can give me some information."

She continued her fixated gaze, slightly raising her perfectly arched brows in expectation.

"I need to get in touch with someone who can make me a fake Nevada driver license."

She threw back her head in amusement and uttered a throaty laugh. "You surely don't think I would be able to do that!"

I could feel my face flushing again in embarrassment. I wasn't sure what to say. I was pretty sure there was no way in hell she would buy my hard luck story.

"No, I don't. But it is imperative that I get one . . . and I was hoping you would know someone who could. . . ."

"What makes you think I would know someone who could do that?" she asked.

I decided honesty would be best—honesty to a certain point, that is.

"I was told by several of the other performance artists, who wish to remain anonymous, that you might be the one who would be able to put me in touch with someone who could get one for me."

I had no idea how she would react to my candor. I feared that I may have totally blown it and that I would have to start all over again trying to find another contact.

Abruptly, she smiled. "Buy me another raki while I think about it."

I signaled the waiter, and after he had brought her another raki, I sat quietly, leaving my wine untouched while she debated whether or not she would help me. Finally, she said, "If I *can* give you the name of someone to get in touch with, it will cost you."

I felt such an overwhelming feeling of relief flooding my body, I almost cried. But I merely said: "Okay."

We sat in silence for a few more minutes while she sipped her raki and continued her contemplation. I didn't move, except for taking quiet, shallow breaths; I didn't want to break her train of thought or do anything else that might cause her to change her mind. Suddenly, in the blink of an eye, she rose to her feet, picked up what was left of her raki, and downed it. "Give me a C-note for my research," she demanded, holding out her hand, "And I will see what I can do to try to get the information you need. Come back in two nights. If I do get the information for you, it will cost you another C-note."

I drew in a deep breath, feeling as if a small weight had been lifted from my shoulders; maybe she actually would be able to help me. Placing a hundred dollar bill in her hand I said, "Yes, I will be here again in two nights with the rest of the money. Thank you." But the last two words were said to her back, as she was already walking away.

Two restless nights later I was back on Fremont Street. At least this time my visit was more purposeful, with hopefully positive results. And since I now knew the area where Jade performed, thankfully, I didn't have to walk up and down the Fremont Street expanse looking for her.

I arrived just as she was finishing setting up. I stood in the background, watching, trying to be unobtrusive. This time she was wearing a silver sequined bra and belt; her skirt consisted of yards of turquoise chiffon embroidered in a delicate design with silver thread. Her drummer was there in his usual place, sitting on a small stool at the edge of the Persian-style rug, with her tip basket next to him. However this time her snake basket was missing. *Perhaps Brian was tired and needed a rest from performing, I mused.* In its place was a red sword case.

She was busy wrapping herself in a large chiffon veil decorated in a variegated design of lavender and turquoise swirls. It covered every part of her except her face. When her music began, her arms snaked gracefully out from inside her veil, playing her finger cymbals. She began with exotic hand gestures, but soon transitioned to swaying arm movements; again, much like a snake. She slowly began to twirl in small circles, removing the veil from her body as she moved. Once the veil was removed, she swirled it, flew it like butterfly wings, spun it, and finally sent it sailing off into the air over her head. She stopped for an instant in a dramatic pose, then began circling round the rug doing fast hip shimmies. Like last time, I found her dance to be mesmerizing.

When she reached the sword case, she swept it up and began spinning rapidly while holding it straight up above her head with both hands. When she stopped spinning, in one dramatic swoop she removed the sword from its case. Placing the sword on her right hip she did several thrusts; then she removed it from her hip and placed it on edge atop her head. She spun around three times, and when she stopped, the sword did two more revolutions before coming to a standstill.

It was dizzying to watch. Finally she knelt on the rug, with the sword still on her head, and began a series of serpentine body rolls, the sword remaining steadfastly in place. I involuntarily shook my head in disbelief that someone could actually do this. Then, in one lithe movement, she removed the sword from her head while rising. She did several fast spins with the sword raised above her head held with both hands, then stopped and bowed. She took a few more bows until the clapping and cheers stopped. I noticed that, once again, her tip basket runneth over with bills, mostly in the larger denominations.

She saw me and nodded, motioning with her head in the direction of the bar where we had gone two nights ago. After retrieving her veil where it had floated down nearby, she gave her drummer a hand signal, picked up her tip basket and followed me.

My heart was pounding in expectation, wondering if she had the information I needed. Once we were seated, I waited, not speaking, while she wrapped her veil around her shoulders. After we had ordered our drinks—her signature raki and I my usual cabernet—she faced me and fixed her eyes on mine. This time we were seated in better light, and I realized that her eyes were actually more like Ubatuba granite: hard, cold, and a very dark green color with lighter golden flecks, rather than the smoky obsidian I had thought at our first meeting. *Contact lenses, I wondered?*

"I have the information you want," she said, snapping me from my conjecturing. "Give me a pencil and paper, along with the C-note, and I will write the name and address for you."

As I reached into my purse and pulled out a pen and a small note pad, which I passed to her, I couldn't help being slightly amused at her continuous use of the term "C-note." Perhaps she has a penchant for old gangster movies, I mused as I discreetly pulled a hundred dollar bill from my wallet. I was careful to make sure she was unable to see how much money I had, while thinking it was good thing I had gone to the bank and gotten plenty of cash before beginning this quest. So far, the Destiny endeavor was costing more than what I had originally anticipated.

While she was writing, our drinks were served. She handed back my pad and pen. "Nice doing business with you," she said. Then she stood, lifted her glass, chugged her raki, and picked up her tip basket, along with the hundred dollar bill.

"Could I ask you one more thing?" I stammered.

"Yes, what is it?"

What are those little cymbals you wear on your fingers called?"

"She gave me that throaty, husky laugh of hers again. "Zills: spelled Z-I-L-L-S!" she answered, already beginning to slither her way back to her performance area. The way she moved really did remind me of a snake—a venomous cobra getting ready to strike! I guess I should have been grateful that she had decided to help me; she just as easily could have decided not to. But even now there was no way of knowing if she really had helped me; I had no guarantee that the information she had given me would turn out to be what I needed. I wouldn't know the answer to that until I checked it out. For a few seconds I had the sinking feeling that she was inwardly chortling at how she had duped some dumb rube into believing that she could get her an illegal Nevada driver license. I wondered if I had just been scammed out of two hundred dollars. Either way, I had no desire to ever see her again!

As I wearily drove home, I couldn't help but wonder what Marc would think of all of this. Somehow I thought he would be proud of my ingenuity, as well as my determined effort to pull myself out of my grief and go on with my life. I could almost feel the warmth of his smile. Two of the many things he used to tell me he loved about me were my quirky imagination and my wry sense of humor. The quirky imagination was still intact; but I was still working on bringing back the wry sense of humor. I couldn't help grinning when I thought of how much he would have loved seeing me in my Destiny garb! Once I was home and in bed, with Hally cuddled next to me, I made a mental note to do a Google search on raki sometime. Who knows: I might even be daring enough to try it.

CHAPTER 3

— • • • —

THE NEXT MORNING, I set out on another try to get Destiny her driver license, hoping that the errand would go smoothly. I was still wondering if Jade had made a fool out of me and if I had wasted two hundred dollars (not counting Jade's tips and the drinks I had bought) on a wild goose chase. As it turned out, Jade had been true to her word. My "contact" had a little rented place, actually little more than the size of a chicken-coop, downtown, not far from Fremont Street. However even though his place was tiny, he seemed to have all of the necessary technical equipment. After haggling over a price, which turned out to be considerably more than I had thought fair, the license process progressed unhindered. He took my picture in my Destiny garb and Photoshopped it onto a Nevada license. The process was quick; I was in and out within twenty minutes.

Unfortunately, being the trusting—and still naïve soul that I am, along with being so relieved and proud of myself for my success, I didn't look closely at the birth date on the license. I was more concerned with my photo and the license's general appearance of authenticity. Several days later, when I found the perfect apartment to rent in Destiny's name, was when I discovered that the little creep had given me a license that had already expired! Luckily, after much pleading, I was able to go ahead and sign the apartment lease with the contingency that I have the license renewed as soon as possible. When I tried to open a checking account in Destiny's name, the bank also would not accept my expired license as ID. This, of course, left me with no choice: I would have to take the friggin' driving test in order to get the license renewed! Damn! Another trip to the DMV! All of that stress all over again!

As you can well imagine, having to take the test put a new wrinkle in the caper—so to speak. Destiny didn't have a vehicle, and a vehicle was necessary in which to take the driving test. I had taken my driving test when I was sixteen, which was during a totally different world than the world that existed today. Therefore I wasn't sure of the ins and outs and type of information that would be required for the test vehicle. In all probability, I would have to provide some kind of proof of insurance and registration.

I didn't want to use my car, or any of my friends' vehicles, nor would it be prudent to use a rented vehicle. I didn't want to use a vehicle that might, in any way, be traced back either to me or to any of the rest of us. I knew the fake license was breaking the law, and I wasn't sure how much else of what we were doing was totally on the right side of the law. I surely did not want any of us to get into trouble just because we wanted to partake in the enjoyment of a possibly more risqué side of life.

I decided to run this new problem by Julie, and, luckily, she was able to come to my rescue. She remembered that she had a past acquaintance who owed her a favor, who just happened to own a used car lot on the other side of the Strip. His name was Rolf, and he agreed to allow us to use one of the cars on his lot, no questions asked.

On the dreaded test day, I carefully applied my makeup, glad that I had recently splurged on getting eyelash extensions. The permanent, individual eyelashes really speeded up getting ready. After putting in my blue contact lenses, I pulled on the Reba wig, fluffing it and tweaking it until I achieved the perfectly tousled look I was striving for. Lastly, I donned the black leather outfit. I scrutinized my reflection in the mirror, making sure that I had achieved what I viewed to be the correct Destiny persona before I left to pick up Julie.

All at once I realized the one good thing to come from all of this hassle was that I hadn't had time to be sad or to fall into my grief pit. For that, I was grateful. Again, I imagined I could feel the warmth of Marc smiling down on me . . . or maybe it wasn't just in my imagination. . . .

Julie and I had agreed on a plan for me to drive the two of us to the car lot in my Jaguar. When Rolf saw us drive up, he rushed out of the office. He was nicely dressed in dark jeans, a long-sleeved white dress shirt and a camel hair blazer, with no tie. His hair was the color of wheat (with no grey!) and looked like he had it expensively styled on a regular basis. He had a diamond stud in his left earlobe. He greeted us with a broad grin, which revealed expensive dental work. *Lumineers, I wondered?*

At first I thought his grin was merely the conditioned sociable grin of the professional salesman. But I soon changed my mind; this time I was sure my intuition was on target. He boldly eyed my cleavage while subconsciously licking his lips. As his grin became what I considered lecherously friendly, I imagined I could picture a distinct image of what was running through his mind: him with Julie and me in a tangled threesome-assignation. I felt my cheeks flushing in embarrassment. He gave the impression of being a smooth, high-roller type, and I wondered under what conditions Julie had known him in the past and why he owed her a favor? My imagination began to run wild, and I made a mental note to ask her sometime.

We decided that I would drive my Jaguar to the DMV with Julie following in the five-year-old "loaded" Lincoln that was to be my driving exam vehicle. It was the car Rolf had decided to lend us, giving us no choice in the selection, and I couldn't help wondering about the car's history. It was what many non Las Vegans might picture as being the perfect "Las Vegas car."

We went to the Henderson DMV this time, which was closest, and many miles away from the location where I had made my first disastrous attempt to obtain a license. I still couldn't help cringing every time I thought of it; I certainly didn't want to take a chance of being remembered by that previous clerk. With my luck, he would turn out to be a roving tester who would be my examiner when my allotted number came up today.

I hadn't bothered studying for the test—which was stupid, I admit. But I never gave it a thought that I might need to. When I barely passed the written part of the exam, I began worrying about what would happen if by some fluke I didn't pass the driving exam. Not only would that be a total embarrassment, but it would also end up creating a complex problem. If I were to flunk, it would not be legal for me to drive in my Destiny guise. Therefore, Julie would have to drive me home in the Lincoln to ditch my Destiny garb. Then she would have to drive me back to the DMV to get my Jaguar so that I could follow her back to the lot to return the Lincoln.

I felt fidgety as I waited my turn and jumped when a male voice behind me said: "Hello." I turned around to see a uniformed man, easily young enough to have been my son, holding a clipboard. He grinned as he introduced himself. "My name is Liam Andrews, and I'll be your examiner."

"Hello, I'm Destiny."

His eyebrows lifted briefly when I said my name. "Well don't be nervous, Destiny," he said, continuing to grin, "I'm sure you'll do just fine."

Once again, I wasn't sure if his grin was in casual friendliness, or if he was hitting on me; I realized as Destiny, my judgment was off. I would need to work on that, I mentally resolved. I had been out of the dating game for a long time. I was also sure that the rules had likely changed a great deal during the years that I had been out.

"Are you an entertainer, Destiny?" he asked, as we made our way to my loaner Lincoln.

"No, Liam, I'm just an ordinary person," I answered. Hoping that would be the end of his personal questions.

I unlocked the car door, and he watched as I slid awkwardly into the driver's seat, my leather skirt accidently hiking up past my mid thighs. I tried to yank it back down while he was climbing into the passenger side.

By the time I was situated behind the wheel with Liam beside me, I was so nervous that my hands were perspiring and my stomach was filled with butterflies. To make matters worse, in addition to being young, he was also attractive. From the tailored uniform shirt he was wearing that showed off his physique, it was obvious that he was a bodybuilder. I wondered if he fancied himself irresistible to women. But maybe I was being too cynical, I thought, and I tried to force myself to relax.

He put me through the standard mechanical issues: lights, windshield wipers, etc., and every time I looked at him, I was afraid I would find him leering at me. By the time he gave me instructions on where to pull out onto the street to actually test my driving skills, my hands were so sweaty that they felt slippery. I gripped the steering wheel tightly, half expecting at any moment to feel his hand on my knee, which made me even more nervous. But, thankfully, he maintained a professional attitude—with the exception of occasional sidewise glances at my Victoria's Secret push-up-bra-enhanced cleavage.

I tend to be a lead-foot driver at times, and I really had to concentrate on watching my speed. I felt like I was doing pretty well when, had it not been for his seatbelt, I probably would have come close to throwing him through the windshield with the quick stop part of the exam. I couldn't help indulging myself in a smug smile.

"Excellent reflexes," he commented.

However, just as I was congratulating myself on a job well done, I nearly lost it on the parallel parking, which was totally mortifying. After several frustratingly embarrassing attempts, I was finally able to cram the loaner Lincoln into that ridiculously small-sized space—which I swear they deliberately make at least six inches smaller than the standard-size automobile! I could feel perspiration uncomfortably dripping down my face (the wig making my head hotter than usual), and trickling between my breasts. I didn't have the courage to look at Liam; I was sure he was smirking.

But, thank God, I passed! And I was soon rewarded with a new license in my hot little hand, with Destiny's photo, in Destiny's name! At last, Destiny Aaron had a bona fide (although illegal!) ID! I felt like I had a pretty good idea of how it must feel to give birth after an excruciatingly long labor.

CHAPTER 4

— • • • —

JULIE AND I were the first to arrive for our luncheon at Maggiano's, with Nikki arriving shortly after. For me it had been a busy three weeks.

"Well, Jayne, have you worked everything out yet?" asked Nikki. "It's difficult for me to imagine how we're going to do this, or what we'll be able to do with Destiny. But I have confidence in you, and I'm looking forward to hearing your ideas."

"I don't think you'll be disappointed . . . at least I hope you won't. But I'll wait until the others get here before I explain everything so I'll only have to go over it once. It tends to be rather detailed."

"I imagine it does," she said, giving me a mischievous grin.

We had reserved a large, circular booth, and when everyone had arrived the nine of us eagerly crowded around the super-size round table. I waited for each of us to get settled and sipping a glass of a favorite beverage before I launched into my dissertation on Destiny—subject for their final approval of the particulars.

I took a hefty swig of my pinot noir and began the lengthy narration of my extremely difficult and intense three-week labor and delivery in giving birth to Destiny:

"After much deliberation, I did decide that it would be best to have Destiny be the original 5'6" tall and weigh 120 pounds that I first mentioned." As I began to hear mutterings that we were all different heights and weights, I raised my hand for silence so I could continue. "Now don't everyone get in a tizzy. This was the median for us; remember, if push should come to shove, we can lie about losing/gaining weight. Destiny will have deep blue eyes and long curly auburn hair; I've already purchased the perfect wig! It did turn out to be in a style similar to the way Reba McEntire wore her hair when it was very long and curly. The eye color I chose is an unusual dark blue violet color. I'll pass around that info so you can all order a pair. Of course each of us will provide our own Destiny wardrobe.

"Unfortunately, since 9/11, it is very difficult to do anything without a picture ID, which is also not an easy thing to get, as I'm sure you all well know. Although criminals seem to be able to easily establish new identities, I had a devil of a time getting Destiny an ID. At times I thought it seemed impossible. You have no idea what I had to go through to get it; but I finally prevailed!

"Not allowing any grass to grow under my feet, the day after our last luncheon was when I found and purchased the wig, along with a new outfit in black leather, something I have never worn before. What a hoot that was, the first time I saw myself in the mirror with my black leather outfit and Destiny's wig. It really did make me feel like I was someone else.

"The next day, I tackled the DMV for a license in Destiny's name. After an interminable wait—you know how long those lines are at the DMV, when it was finally my turn, it did not go well. I tried to play on the male clerk's sympathy with what I thought was a viable hard luck story—embellished with lots of eye batting and woeful pleading of having recently moved here from Florida and losing all of my identification when my purse was stolen shortly after my arrival. Then when the clerk said they could contact the Florida DMV to obtain a copy of my license, I had to do some fast ad-libbing."

As I continued my tale of relating my hard luck story to the DMV clerk, snickers began to break out.

"Yeah, yeah, I know. Actually, I wish you all could have been there to witness my agony. It was not a pretty sight! It turned out to be a complete bungle, and, unfortunately, it left me back at square one and having to start all over again."

"What did you do?" asked Nikki?

"At first I didn't know how to proceed; I had to do a good bit of re-thinking. I finally decided that I would have to find a way to get a fake license. And, since I'm not acquainted with any unsavory people who could do that for me, after conferring with Julie, we thought the most likely opportunity to get what I needed would be found on Fremont Street."

This revelation elicited much eye-rolling and more snickers, which grew in intensity as I described my Fremont Street exploits. Most of them had not been to Fremont Street for a number of years.

"I was forced to prowl the area for three nights in a row before I found an interesting someone, who suggested an even more interest-ing someone—both of whom shall remain nameless—who could put me in touch with someone who could get me a fake license! Then two more anxious nights before I could get the name of the 'intouchee,' who had a little rented place near the Fremont Street area. He took my picture with me dressed as Destiny and Photoshopped it onto a license. However I didn't realize until I tried to open a checking account in Destiny's name, using it for ID, that the little worm had given me a license that had expired the previous month! Naturally, being expired, it wasn't accepted to open the bank account or to rent an apartment, which meant I had to take the damned driver's test to get it renewed!"

Since this drew a round of laughter, it gave me a chance to stop long enough for another hefty slug of wine. I couldn't help but notice that all eyes were on me, rapt with anticipation for the rest of my story.

As I continued my narration, their reactions ranged from head shaking, to more eye-rolling and a few chuckles. When I got to the part of admitting that I had not studied for the license exam, my con-fession resulted in another flurry of laughter.

"OK, OK, enough! How many of YOU could pass the driving exam now without studying? I just want you to know what I had to go through to get Destiny's license. And that was just the beginning!"

I continued with a detailed account of my driving test, along with a description of my examiner, having to stop several times for their laughter to die down. By the time I got to the parallel parking fiasco they were nearly rolling on the floor with hilarity.

"But," I said loudly, over the laughter, "I persevered on, even though at times it was a humiliating experience. And, I passed! I am now proud to announce that—due to the identity bestowed by this hard-earned, newly issued Nevada driver license (which I held up for all to see)—Destiny Aaron is officially born!"

The laughter stopped and was immediately replaced with a spontaneous round of applause; I paused and gave an exaggerated bow before continuing on.

"With a cash deposit, I opened a checking account in Destiny's name at a bank branch that should be large enough to enable her to remain anonymous. Remember, we won't establish an email account; therefore we won't be able to do any banking online. We don't want any kind of personal connection that could be traced to any of us—just to be on the safe side. Of course, getting Destiny's required Social Security number presented another brief problem, which after some careful thought I feel I was able to satisfactorily resolve. Rather than arriving at the Social Security number by choosing numbers at random, which could conceivably cause future problems by actually belonging to someone, I felt safe in using my late grandmother's number. And, for my sensational finale of this saga, I will end with this special surprise: I rented a one-bedroom apartment several miles from the Strip, paying the deposit and first month's rent in cash! Because of a promotional deal, I was able to get a large reduction in the rent by signing a year's lease."

This provoked a few disapproving mumbles, and I waved my hand so I could defend my decision. "Since I am relatively sure that we will most likely be using the apartment indefinitely if Destiny proves to be a success, I decided that this was the best way to go. And, although it is not the usual way I do business, if we should decide that we no longer want to play with our alter ego, well, we can just walk away from the lease. Since Destiny doesn't actually exist, there is no way any of us can be hurt financially."

I paused to allow what I had explained so far to be digested and to reply to any possible comments/questions. But none were forthcoming. It appeared everyone had been stunned into silence . . . speechlessness would probably be a more appropriate term.

Nikki was the first to comment. "Wow, Jayne, we already knew you had a wild imagination, but that story is over the top! I guess sometimes it does come in handy to have that kind of an imagination. No wonder you're a writer."

I finished what was left in my wine glass, waiting for the verbal deluge from the rest of the group. However no one else spoke. Finally, they began to look around at one another, then at me, but continued to remain mute. Maybe we were all a little overwhelmed at the idea of what we were doing. Maybe in some ways it was even a little bit scary.

I finally broke the silence. "Well, do you all still want to carry on with this?

Suddenly the group came alive with a buzz of excitement as the realization began to sink in. We were actually going to be able to play with assuming a different identity, acting out our fantasies each in our own, individual way. They could hardly wait to see the license—particularly the way Destiny's picture looked. I had intentionally tilted my head slightly downward when the photo was snapped in order to have less of my face showing. I had also worn the proper height heels to make me exactly 5'6" tall. As I passed Destiny's license around the table, I concluded my monologue with the suggestion that we each contribute an equal amount for Destiny's maintenance on a monthly basis, rather like club dues.

Deena laughed. "Wow, I hardly know what to say! You *have* been busy! I didn't realize how much would be involved. But, no, since we've come this far, I definitely want to continue."

The others, probably still in a bit of shock, also voiced their agreement.

"What's our next step?" asked Nikki.

"Well, now we'll just have to work out more details, including figuring out financial arrangements. I'm glad you all still want to carry on with this, because I did sort of stick my neck out when I signed the year's lease on the apartment! And, as I mentioned before, pay a security deposit and the first month's rent. I hope to be reimbursed for my expenses thus far, including the deposits I had to pay for electricity and water. I also set up a cable bundle deal for monthly landline phone, television, and internet service with Wi-Fi. The fee and incidentals for the driver license will be my contribution. We're going to have to total up the sum we'll need each month for rent and utilities. Whatever else Destiny needs, I guess we'll discover as we go along. Julie helped me prepare a spreadsheet copy for each of you of my itemized expenses to date, along with a suggestion of monthly dues."

After looking over the figures, they all agreed that the costs so far were reasonable, which was a relief. Although, thankfully, Marc had left me well-provided for financially, so far the expense of establishing Destiny's identity had run quite a bit out of pocket—more than I had anticipated. I resumed my summary of the expenses breakdown: "The cost of electricity and water should be minimal, since the apartment would not be used on a daily, 24-hour basis."

We finally settled on monthly dues in an amount we thought would be more than enough to cover essentials. After a short discussion, we decided to collect the "dues" at our luncheons, and we would take turns, dressed as Destiny, making the cash deposits in person to Destiny's checking account. That way, we should be able to maintain our anonymity since the apartment rent, phone and other monthly utilities would be paid by automatic deductions from Destiny's checking account.

I have some furniture in storage that I can contribute toward furnishing the apartment," offered Chloe.

"Oh, that's a great idea," exclaimed Nikki. "I bet among us we have enough to furnish Destiny with quite a comfortable abode."

The others murmured unanimous approval of the suggestion.

"When do we get to see this apartment—and the wig?" asked Tiffani. "We all need to try on the wig!"

"As soon as we finish eating," I answered. "That's one reason I wanted to rent something close to the Strip—so it would be more convenient, since that is the area where Destiny will most likely be carrying out her various escapades."

Needless to say we made short work of finishing our lunch. I led the way in a caravan of luxury autos driving to Destiny's apartment, with all of us experiencing a goodly amount of our old high school exhilaration!

CHAPTER 5

—— • • • ——

THE APARTMENT WAS a small, one-bedroom, one-and-a-half bath unit in a newly renovated, four-story complex. It fronted on a side street with little traffic and had a covered parking garage on one side. There was no doorman, which would help protect our anonymity. Instead, the front entrance utilized a keypad for security. The first floor contained an attractive front lobby, workout room, sauna, indoor swimming pool, and a meeting room for special events. Our apartment was on the second floor looking out onto the street.

Except for the bedroom, which was carpeted, all of the flooring in the unit had been laid with large porcelain tiles in a grey teak-stone design, with light grey grout. The bedroom carpeting was a plush, pale grey pile that complimented the tiles. The kitchen contained white cabinets and a huge island with an overhang on one side that could be used as a breakfast bar. Off the kitchen was a small closet that held a stacked washer and dryer. All of the counter tops, including the bathrooms, were white quartz, with a white, subway tiled backsplash in a herringbone pattern in the kitchen. After a flurry of exploration accompanied by oohs and aahs, everyone gave the apartment high marks.

Although it was unfurnished, we decided it wouldn't take much to accommodate our needs. We made a list of the furnishings and housewares each of us could contribute, and decided to shop at some of the consignment and second hand stores for the rest of the necessities. For starters, we needed a king-size mattress and box springs, which

Cassandra said she could supply. We also needed a dresser, couch, coffee table, several upholstered chairs, and bar stools. Nikki said she could provide a small dinette table with 4 chairs.

"Now for the fun part," I said, as I pulled the wig out of my tote bag. The initial response included frowns and questionable head shaking from a few, with grins of favorable approval from the rest.

"It's so outlandish! Much too flamboyant!" complained Chloe.

"Just wait until I model it," I said, as I hurried into the bathroom. After pulling it onto my head and tucking in my longish blonde hair and doing some style tweaking, I stepped back into the living room. I was greeted by some audible gasps, followed seconds later by spontaneous clapping as a show of praise in my choice of the wig. They were amazed at how much it changed my appearance.

"Well, I have to say I was wrong!" admitted Chloe.

I gave her a quick smile and a nod in acknowledgement.

"The apartment will be our base of operation," I explained. "We can leave the wig and our individual Destiny apparel here, along with her identification . . . and, well, if any of us should decide to do any entertaining as Destiny, we could also do that here."

My last statement seemed to catch some unaware. They stared at me, unsure of my meaning until it suddenly dawned on them. Others immediately raised eyebrows and smiled at the scenario in their minds, my meaning being quite clear.

"How soon can we begin and how will we decide who gets to be Destiny, and when?" asked Deena, excitedly? "In case you haven't guessed, I'm ready to try it out as soon as possible!"

"Well, what do you all think? Should we draw numbers?" I asked, taking a small notebook from my purse.

"That sounds fair," said Nikki.

And the others nodded their approval.

"Just leave me out of the drawing. I'll take my Destiny turn last—or whenever someone else doesn't want to have a turn," said Kayla.

I tore several sheets from the notebook, in turn tearing them into eight smaller pieces and numbering them one through eight, then folding them. Since we didn't have a bowl from which to draw, I placed them in a pile on the floor and we each took turns stirring them around. However we were still undecided as to who would get to draw first, and what order to follow afterwards.

"Why don't we go with age?" suggested Nikki, "With the oldest going first, then the next oldest, and so on."

"Yeah, Nikki, that would be fine for you, since you're the oldest," scoffed Amber good-naturedly, who was the youngest.

"Is Nikki's suggestion agreeable with everyone?" I asked, anxious to draw my number since I was the second oldest. "Remember, the order in which we draw really isn't that important. It is the number we end up with that will decide when we get to be Destiny."

Each of us picked up one of the small folded wads, some smiling, while others scowled as the selected numbers were revealed.

"Well, what's the order?" I asked, reasonably pleased with my number "four."

"I'm first," exclaimed Cassandra! "Does that mean I can do it tonight if I want?"

"Um, I guess, unless we need to work out more details anyone can think of. Of course the apartment won't be furnished yet, if that matters to you."

"Well, I can't wait any longer to try this on," said Julie, snatching up the wig and hurrying to the powder room.

"I want to try it on, too," said Deena running after her, followed by the others.

"Surprisingly, I'm even getting caught up in this madness!" confessed Kala when she took her turn trying on the wig.

After we had all had a turn, giggling and marveling at how the wig changed each one's appearance, I jotted down the schedule, listing the order in which each of us would have our first night of being Destiny.

"I guess down the line we won't need to stay in strict order. Just be sure to check with me first. I'll keep a schedule to make sure there are no double bookings. Oh, and don't forget, if you don't already have some, order your deep blue violet contact lenses as soon as possible. It could be important if someone should ever decide to closely examine Destiny's ID for any reason!"

However at the time, that seemed a very remote possibility. "We'll keep her driver license, debit card, and any future credit cards—should we ever decide to get any—in a wallet, which we'll leave here at the apartment. Just don't forget to take it along with you on your nights as Destiny," I cautioned.

We agreed to "up" our luncheon get-togethers to once a week from now on. And after I had given out an apartment key and a copy of the entry code to everyone, we parted with an air of jubilance I was sure none of us had experienced for many years! Expectation lit our eyes, perhaps even rivaling the Vegas casino lights in the intensity of their brightness!

CHAPTER 6

———— • • • ————

WHEN WE MET again a week later to see how the Destiny Club was working out, I had already taken my turn. In fact, during the previous seven nights the first five of us on the schedule had already taken a turn. Although I had enjoyed my first stint as Destiny, I had felt more inhibited and self-conscious than what I had thought. Perhaps I was just not ready yet to flirt and meet men, even under the protection of a different persona; however I hoped I would become less timid as I continued with my turns. I had thought Destiny could be the impetus I needed in being able to move on with my life, which I knew Marc would want me to do. But I wasn't sure how much he would approve of me moving on as Destiny, rather than just being myself.

As we began to compare notes, the last four on the list, Julie, Chloe, Deena, and, yes, even Kayla, were envious and looking forward to their night of being Destiny.

We were lunching at the Border Grill at Mandalay Bay this time; but again, the excellent food took a back seat to Destiny. Cassandra confided that she had enjoyed a wild time with her debut as Destiny. "I haven't had that much fun in years! I might even have decided to entertain at the apartment had it been furnished. Men couldn't pay enough attention to me. I can't wait to do it again! So come on, gals, let's get that apartment furnished and decorated!"

It wasn't difficult to imagine men paying attention to Cassandra, even without her Destiny guise. She has a petite, curvy figure, with long, naturally wavy blonde hair. She has an innocent baby face, with large, expressive brown eyes. With her vibrant personality, as Destiny, she must be a knockout!

"Well, I had fun too, added Nikki, tossing her shoulder-length, chestnut hair, "but not nearly as wild a time as you apparently had, Cassandra. I guess I'm more inhibited. Being single probably makes a difference; I would feel guilty even talking to other men. I know how hurt I would feel if my husband flirted with some other woman when I wasn't around. I just had a nice dinner and did a little gambling. But I did enjoy the interested looks I got from some very attractive men."

Nikki is one of those women who is a natural beauty; she has such perfect features she needs little makeup. She attracts plenty of interested looks without the Destiny enhancements. Therefore I could only imagine how stunning she must be as Destiny.

As the others related their experiences, I envisioned how differently each would look in their Destiny disguises.

"I also thoroughly enjoyed my time," offered Amber, who had been third on the list. "Several men offered to buy me drinks, and one asked me to blow on the dice for luck. Then another wanted me to stand next to him to bring him luck in blackjack. They both generously rewarded me with part of their winnings afterwards. It was fun gambling with someone else's money. But that was as far as I went."

I could completely understand men being attracted to Amber. She has a casual, out-going demeanor, and the lithe, muscular body of a natural athlete, which she was. She had been a champion swimmer in high school. She wears her platinum blonde hair in a pixie cut; and her eyes are baby blue. The Destiny guise would be a total turn around for her.

"Mine was also pretty tame," admitted Tiffani, with a grin. "But my first time was kind of a test run to see just how far I want to go and what I want to do while playing my new wicked twin role."

Tiffani is probably the most exotic looking of the group, having inherited the mixed heritage of her Mexican-American mother and

African-American father, with a café au lait skin tone and high cheek-bones. Her almond-shaped eyes are dark brown. She wears her waist-length dark brown hair pulled back in a low ponytail. As Destiny, she would look even more exotic.

"My evening was mostly like yours, Amber and Nikki," I added. "I guess I also don't have the nerve that you do, Cassandra."

"Well, you four just wait," admonished Cassandra with a wicked chuckle. "You may change your attitude when you realize the potential here."

When we met again the following week, by then all of us had en-joyed a turn, with Cassandra already having had a second time. The others had also relished their nights as Destiny, but hadn't been par-ticularly daring.

"Just to get out by myself as someone else was rejuvenating. I wasn't someone's wife, mother, etc., I was me," disclosed Deena. I enjoyed an excellent, unhurried dinner without having to worry about pleasing anyone other than myself. I apologize for any doubts I had about this idea in the beginning."

Deena is tall, with a toned body. Her straight, mahogany-colored hair is several inches below her shoulders. Her bangs cut straight across her forehead enhance her eyes, which, without the blue tinted contact lenses are a natural deep green color. She is striking with or without the Destiny garb.

"Well, now that I've had my second turn as Destiny, I have to say I continued to enjoy the complimentary looks I got from men," Cassandra stated bluntly. "And I don't mind saying it, either! In fact, surprisingly, I was tempted to allow myself to get friendly with one man whom I found particularly attractive. He was a real hottie, but young! So of course, I didn't!" She said, giggling. I wondered if she was being entirely honest.

I turned to Kayla, who has very short, dark curly hair that perfectly frames her heart-shaped face. She has large hazel eyes and a sexy, pouty smile. She is what I would describe in a word: cute! Her Destiny guise would be a drastic change.

"What about you, Kayla, what did you do with your night of being Destiny?

She blushed, then in a low voice, she haltingly confessed, "Well . . . I even enjoyed my turn. . . ." She paused for a few seconds, then broke into a teasing grin. "But I'm not going to tell you what I did. I'll just tell you that it was deliciously naughty, and . . . that's all."

We acknowledged her contribution with surprise, quickly followed by a volley of questions. But after much wheedling, when she stubbornly refused to elaborate, the conversation momentarily stalled.

Finally Julie broke the lull. "Well, like Kayla, I also enjoyed my turn. And although I wasn't 'deliciously naughty' like you, Kayla, I did have a fabulous time. And I *will* tell you what I did. I went to one of the casinos with live-band dancing, and I danced my feet off," her deep-set, smoky blue eyes became more animated as she continued. "I had forgotten how much I love dancing. It was wonderful! What a welcome diversion Destiny is to my life!"

I could picture Julie dancing her feet off; even without her Destiny attire, Julie is gorgeous: Tall and curvy, with long, sun-streaked blonde hair.

"Well, I know I'm readily looking forward to my next night as Destiny," proclaimed Nikki, picking up the conversation again. "I thoroughly enjoyed myself, even if I also wasn't 'deliciously naughty' like you, Kayla, or as daring as you, Cassandra."

"I can't believe we're really doing this and it's actually working!" exclaimed Deena, laughing. "I still keep wondering when the other shoe is going to drop. I can't help thinking this might end up with one, some, or all of us in trouble. But I guess if that happens we'll figure a way out of it; heck, we were always able to do that in high school, and we're considerably more mature and wiser now than we were then."

"You worry too much," criticized Cassandra.

I realized that Chloe was the only one who hadn't had a chance yet to tell us about her Destiny night. "What about you, Chloe? You're the only one of us who hasn't shared her Destiny experience."

Chloe is the most petite of the bunch and usually the most introverted member of the group. She wears her chin-length, copper-colored hair in a very chic bob. She is also probably the most sophisticated of the group in her dress and demeanor. She has a flawless complexion and her makeup is always impeccably applied. As well as being the most introverted member of the group, she is also probably the most conservative. As I pictured how differently she must have looked in her Destiny attire, I couldn't help wondering if it had also drastically changed her persona, and if it had, to what degree.

She gave a shy smile as she said, "Oh, it was pretty much routine. I enjoyed myself the same as the rest of you."

"But, Chloe, some of us 'enjoyed' ourselves more than others," commented Amber.

"I just ate a nice dinner, gambled a little, and then went home," she answered, averting her eyes. We all noticed with surprise that Chloe was blushing. She seemed so ill at ease that none of us pursued the subject further. Perhaps after having had her turn, she found the Destiny Club distasteful and was having second thoughts, but was continuing to go along with the group as a good sport. She had certainly seemed as enthusiastic as the rest of us in the beginning. Maybe she was just a more private person than we had previously realized and was uncomfortable sharing personal details with the rest of the group.

The following weekend we welcomed the beginning of the month of April by meeting at the apartment, each of us bringing along our hodge-podge of collected items for furnishing Destiny's home. Cassandra had arranged to have the bed delivered earlier in the week, and I had found a slate grey suede couch with two matching chairs at a consignment store, which were delivered yesterday. As I had hoped, the couch and chairs contrasted nicely with the lighter grey floor tiles. Today, I had brought a landline phone with an answering machine. There were three phone jacks in the apartment, and I chose the one on the kitchen backsplash to plug in the phone.

In the back of her Range Rover, Nikki had brought the dinette table, a white concrete pedestal with a glass top, along with four chairs upholstered in sage green suede. After we had helped her unload, we stocked the cupboards with our various contributions of dishes and glassware and made up the bed. At a thrift shop, I had found a white, down comforter with matching pillow shams, and several poufy toss pillows in white and dark grey. Deena surprised us by bringing in a flat screen TV, which we put in the living room. Even though the apartment still needed a few more accessories, which we would add later, it was now cozy and inviting. The important thing was that it was now comfortable for any use, including entertaining "guests" if any of us so desired.

Most of us had brought along wine, and I had brought two bottles of champagne for christening Destiny's new abode. After giving everyone the landline phone number and default answering machine pin, we popped the corks on both of the bottles of champagne. With a loud cheer, we celebrated our decorating achievement with numerous toasts.

CHAPTER 7

———— • • • ————

ALTHOUGH WE HAD always looked forward to our luncheons together, now they had taken on a new importance. We enjoyed being regaled with the intimate tales of Destiny adventures shared by the ones of us who were more daring, with some of us taking turns more often than others. Cassandra seemed to be having the most fun playing with our "evil twin." She had even progressed to entertaining gentlemen in the apartment, which none of the rest of us had done, yet—or at least admitted to having done. None of us were ever judgmental of another's actions, even though individually we might have different ideas of what we considered appropriate for our own private Destiny behavior. To paraphrase a popular saying: to each her own.

Everyone was in agreement that Destiny was like a welcome breath of fresh air having come into our lives; all except me. I hadn't found the fulfillment that I had sought and thought I would find. Having a nice dinner at one of the high-end restaurants, alone, just made me depressed that I wasn't sharing a romantic dinner with Marc. I certainly didn't want to fall back into my grief depression. So next I tried spending my Destiny evenings at the apartment, now that it was decorated and cozy. But no matter what I did, reading, watching a movie or writing on my laptop, I would soon find myself becoming bored and antsy.

By now, two months had passed since the inception of Destiny. The weather was turning warmer, with hot temperatures looming in the very near future. Several days after my last night as Destiny, I decided to treat myself to an afternoon spa treatment. Afterwards, as I was leaving, feeling somewhat rejuvenated, I spotted an array of advertising circulars on a table near the door. I started glancing through them, and one in particular caught my attention. It was an advertisement for pole dancing. Oddly, I found the idea fascinating. Before I could change my mind, I took out my cell phone and called the number on the circular.

The woman I talked to was also the teacher. I made arrangements to attend a class on my Destiny night next week. When I arrived, in my Destiny wig and makeup, but wearing a black leotard and tights, as was requested for the lesson, I was starting to have doubts. I wondered what in the heck I was doing? Although I had studied ballet and modern dancing when I was younger, I was in my forties and not in the best athletic shape. I started having visions of myself whirling around on the pole, upside down, landing on my head and ending up with a concussion. The only thing that kept me from leaving was my thought of how much Marc would have approved of me embarking on this new adventure. I know he would have enjoyed watching me pole dance, and I felt a brief stab of regret that I hadn't done something like this while he was alive. I took a deep breath and resolved to give it the best try I could.

Thankfully, the other five ladies in the class were also amateurs; some were in much worse athletic shape than I. The instructor, Arlene, was patient, and actually was a very good teacher. She went slowly with us and was complimentary of even the smallest accomplishment. She gave us a demonstration of what she planned for us to master if we kept on with the class. I was both intimidated and impressed.

First, she started each of us off with a turn of holding onto the pole and walking around it. After several times of doing that, we did it to music. The music made a huge difference, at least for me it did; it made me feel more graceful and lithe. Attending in my Destiny persona also helped: it freed me from some of my inhibitions. I don't think I would have ever had the courage to do pole dancing without my Destiny guise.

I was grateful that I now had something productive and fulfilling to do on my Destiny nights. As I continued the lessons, I learned not only how to walk around the pole, but how to actually swing and twirl around the pole with a certain amount of grace. We transitioned from doing it barefoot to doing it in two-inch heels, then in 4-inch heels. After six weeks, I had actually learned to wrap my leg around the pole at my knee and spin around it. I imagined Marc applauding and cheering me in the background. In a way, I was doing this for both of us. And so far, I hadn't suffered even one injury, other than sore muscles. Although I was proud of my accomplishment, I made the decision that I wouldn't tell the others about my pole dancing just yet. For now, it would be my secret—mine and Marc's.

As participation in the Destiny Club progressed, we added more personal touches to the apartment: a coffee table and a sage green area rug in the living room, toss pillows on the sofa in sage green and pale turquoise; some herb plants in the kitchen and a large potted palm in the living room; a few small pieces of inexpensive sculpture; some paintings in the living room and bedroom, and a large Matisse print in the powder room. Destiny's apartment now nearly resembled a well-staged model home. In fact, we found it to be so cozy and inviting that it had become a private refuge for us where we could just spend time to reflect and relax, alone, on a Destiny night, savoring the peace and quiet. On nights when I took a break from my pole dancing lessons, I now often went there to write—this time finding the words flowing across the screen of my laptop. Others used the apartment for different purposes. But for whatever reason we chose, it was there for us when we needed it. It didn't take long for the closet to be filled with a sensationally whimsical Destiny wardrobe in our various sizes, reflecting our individual personal tastes. In truth, we were having the time of our lives . . . that is *until the murders began!*

CHAPTER 8

• • •

I<small>T WAS NOW</small> the middle of June, and The Destiny Club had been in operation for over three months when the first body was discovered. The victim, a middle-aged man visiting from Chicago, had been found bludgeoned to death in an alley east of the Strip. But those things happened occasionally, especially in "Sin City." Every town has some kind of homicide rate: the larger the city, usually the higher the rate. And the Las Vegas Metropolitan area is well over two million. Mind you, I'm not making excuses for not paying more attention at the time. I expect that most people don't pay close attention to indiscriminate homicides in their cities, unless acquainted with the victim, or the homicide happens to be of a salacious or sensational nature.

We still didn't pay particular attention to the second homicide three weeks later. It was another middle-aged male, also from out of town, who had been staying in one of the Strip casino/hotels. His body had been found in a seedy area not far from downtown. It wasn't until the third homicide with strange similarities occurring two weeks later did I take notice. I was leisurely enjoying my first cup of morning coffee, contentedly contemplating how I would spend my day, when the newspaper article caught my attention.

The headline suggested a serial killer was at loose. Out of curiosity, I began to skim the article, experiencing a vague sense of unease. But my unease was merely due to the usual feeling of horror invoked when an unbalanced murderer is on the loose, killing at random. Even as I began to read further, my vague feeling of horror still seemed remote to my immediate personal life.

All of the victims had been middle-aged men; all of them had been out of town visitors staying at various hotels located on the Strip—none of which concerned me. Although they had all been staying on the Strip, their bodies had been discovered in different areas of the city. Then something made me stop and go back to reread more carefully. It seemed all of the victims on the evenings preceding their respective murders had the common tie of being seen in the company of an attractive woman, described as having long, curly, auburn hair. One witness recalled hearing the woman's name, but was unable to remember exactly what it was . . . only that it began with the letter "D," and it "was something unusual—maybe Desiree." Presently the auburn-haired woman was not termed a suspect, but was referred to as a person of interest; Metro was asking for the woman to come forward on her own, or for any information that might lead to her identity.

Suddenly I felt sick. The newspaper slipped from my fingers and fell to the floor. I found it hard to grasp what I had just read. Surely it was a mistake! I took a deep breath as my stomach tightened uncomfortably. The room seemed to tilt, and I closed my eyes as a wave of nausea washed over me. I needed to calm myself. I was jumping to conclusions. My mind began to race: *Surely the article couldn't be referring to Destiny . . . that was too preposterous to even consider! I was certain none of us was a murderer. It had to be coincidence. There were lots of women fitting that description; Las Vegas was full of them! The woman they were looking for was probably a call girl.*

Although prostitution is illegal in Las Vegas, it is legal in Nevada, and it still occurs in Las Vegas on a discreet level. I wondered if any of the others had read the article? With trembling fingers, I punched in Julie's phone number.

After ten rings I was about to hang up when she finally answered.

"This better be good, Jayne, to wake me so early."

"Julie, have you read the paper this morning?

"Of course not. My eyes aren't even open yet. How could I read anything when my eyes aren't open?"

She began mumbling, nonsensically, still half asleep, and I hated that I had to wake her up. But I felt she had to know what was in the paper.

"Well, get up and make yourself some coffee and read it, NOW—the article about the serial killer. Then call me right back!"

When I hung up the phone, I realized my hands were shaking. I tried to convince myself that I was overreacting and that when Julie called back she would reassure me that there was nothing to worry about. I tried to calm myself by making a cup of tea. While waiting for it to brew, I picked up the Destiny schedule, anxiously drumming my fingers on the cherry table top as I studied it. Even though I was expecting Julie's call, I still jumped when the phone rang.

"Well?" I answered, after glancing at the Caller-ID to make sure it was Julie.

She now sounded wide-awake. "Geez, Jayne, you don't think one of us murdered those men, do you? I mean, none of us would do something like that, would we? Who was Destiny on the evenings those men were murdered?"

"That's just what I'm checking on now. Let's see . . . Chloe was Destiny the night before the first victim was found, but no one was on the schedule for the other nights . . . unless someone was Destiny and didn't let me know. But that can't be right, either, because even if we don't always stick to a schedule, if someone wants to be Destiny on a certain night she lets me know so there won't be any conflicts or problems. It just doesn't make sense. It's got to be some weird coincidence. But maybe we should put the Destiny Club on hold until this thing is resolved . . . what do you think?"

"Oh, I agree, Jayne! No sense taking any chances, although I'm sure the murders are completely unrelated to Destiny. Good grief, I mean . . . we've all known each other for too many years for one of us to be a murderer. We all have our quirks, but I hardly think any of us could ever do something like that! Besides, what possible motive would any of us have?"

"I know. And I don't think any of us are strong enough to lug bodies around to various parts of the city. The victims were all found a good distance from the Strip. But to be on the safe side, we'll just suspend the Destiny club for a while, either until the murderer is caught or until the murders stop. For all we know, maybe they already have stopped. Maybe there won't be any more. However, if there is another murder, hopefully there won't be any mention of someone matching Destiny's description in the company of the victim on the night of his demise. . . . Or if there is, we will know for certain that it's some other woman, not one of us. Then we can resurrect Destiny and go on with our fun. The only thing . . . what if the murderer is someone who genuinely does look like our Destiny?"

"Now that would be something. . . ."

We divided the others between us, with me calling four and Julie the other three to let them know of the Destiny Club's temporary suspension. This took most of the rest of the day for me, as I expect it also did for Julie, having to explain about the serial killings and what was in the newspaper about a woman described as resembling our Destiny. Although Cassandra was the only one of the group who had read about the killings, she hadn't connected the description of the woman to our Destiny. All were in agreement that suspending the club temporarily was the prudent thing to do. Of course any of us could still use the apartment whenever we desired, just not as Destiny.

The others who hadn't read about the killings seemed so shocked when I explained the reason we were temporarily stopping our Destiny escapades, it reassured me of their innocence. I was now convinced, more than ever, that the murders could have no connection to us. The description and name of the woman had to be purely coincidental. I almost felt silly now about my overreaction. Oh, well, I reasoned, always better to err on the side of caution.

At our next luncheon, we all acknowledged how much we missed Destiny. She had grown to become almost like another member of our group and had taken over a large part of our lives. This was the first luncheon in three months where we weren't able to amuse one another with our various Destiny antics. Destiny had really spiced up our lives!

"Well, hopefully, soon Las Vegas' finest will solve these serial killings, make an arrest, and we can get back to playing with Destiny. Until then, we'll just have to suffer," stated Nikki, with resignation.

While the others were adding their input, I mentally detached myself and began to assess the emotional stability of each of them, with as much objectivity as I could. As my eyes made the rounds, studying each of their faces, I concluded that it had to be impossible for one of us to be a murderer. It was totally unthinkable . . . in fact, almost laughable to even consider. I breathed a sigh of relief as I joined the others in the indulgence of our usual rich desserts.

After another three weeks had passed with no more murders, we decided it was once again safe to resume our secret club. Since "Destiny withdrawal" had been severe, we were all anxious to have a turn as soon as possible; therefore, to be fair, we drew numbers again to re-establish the schedule.

It was an early morning two weeks later, after all of us had experienced at least one more night of being Destiny, when the phone roused me from a particularly delightful slumber. I had been immersed in one of those rare, extraordinary dreams that make perfect sense even though not based on reality. Marc and I were on a romantic cruise, similar to the one we took for our honeymoon, and I resented that someone had rudely interrupted before the dream was able to reach its inevitable romantic climax. I was so ecstatically into the dream, it was particularly jarring to be crashed so abruptly back to my painful reality of being without Marc. My irritation showed in my voice when I answered.

"Yeah, hello," I muttered.

"I'm sorry, Jayne. I probably woke you, but I had to call." It was Julie, and she sounded upset—which caused a brief feeling of guilt at my irritation seconds earlier.

I squinted at the clock. It was only 7:15. "What's wrong, Julie?" I asked in alarm, fearing that something had happened to someone in her family or to one of our group. I knew she wouldn't have called this early unless it was extremely important. Neither of us was seldom up at this time without a very good reason!

"Have you seen the newspaper this morning or the television news?" she asked breathlessly. "There's been another murder!" she exclaimed without waiting for my reply. "The body was found last night, only this time at Red Rock Canyon. According to Metro, it had been there for several days—maybe longer."

I sat up, propping pillows behind me. "No!" It was more an utterance of denial than an answer to her question. I was breathing fast and my head was spinning. I tried to will myself to calm down and clear my mind. After a long pause, I asked, crossing my fingers for luck, "Was there any mention this time of a connection with Destiny?"

"Unfortunately, yes. That's why I'm so upset. A bartender at one of the older casinos on the Strip remembered seeing the victim with a woman matching Destiny's description one evening last week. However Metro won't be able to set the time of death to see if it was on the same night as the murder until after the autopsy. To make matters worse, according to Metro, they are close to establishing the identity of the 'mysterious woman.'" Julie's voice had steadily risen in pitch, her words now tumbling out so rapidly it was as if she were unable to stop; but then, suddenly, she did stop. She took a shuddering breath that was amplified through the telephone receiver.

My body felt numb. "My God, Julie, I just can't believe it! This time it does seem like too much of a coincidence, don't you think? I mean, I just don't know what to think. I still can't believe that one of us could be a cold-blooded killer! It's just not possible!"

"I know! I can't believe it either. I keep thinking it has to be some kind of dreadful coincidence . . . but how? You don't think Metro has connected Destiny to any of us, do you? What if they start contacting us? What will we tell them?"

"Geez, I don't know!" I felt tears stinging my eyes, along with the sudden resurgence of the old familiar feelings of sadness and depression that I had been trying to fight off since losing Marc. I was wishing I had never thought up this crazy idea of the Destiny Club. I should have foreseen that it could lead to trouble. "It's all my fault, you know," I said, my voice tremulous as I tried to fight back tears. "If I'd never mentioned this idiotic fantasy to the rest of you, we'd all still be leading safe, normal lives."

"It's not your fault, Jayne. I clearly remember that no one had to twist any of our arms to do this. And we've had a darned good time with it! If one of us is a serial killer, which I still can't believe, then it had nothing to do with Destiny. Heck, maybe one of us has been knocking off people for years and it was just never discovered—until now."

"Thanks, Julie, for trying to make me feel better. But until this thing is solved, I will feel like I opened a Pandora's Box and unleashed a plague."

"Well, knowing you, I'm not surprised that you feel that way, but you shouldn't. We'd better call the others now and let them know we're disbanding the club again. I just can't seem to get past the possibility that one of us could have murdered those men!"

"I know," I said softly. "Me either."

After we hung up, I succumbed to the crying session that I had been fighting back, or more aptly, my sobbing session. Other than the moment when I had learned that Marc was gone, I couldn't remember when I had felt such despair. I couldn't bear the thought that perhaps one of my dearest friends was a serial killer, and that I was responsible for the deaths of those men. And here I had mistakenly believed that being so focused in creating the Destiny Club was such great grief therapy. It would almost be laughable if it weren't so tragic. Had I been selfish in my zealousness to throw myself into something where I would be so involved that I would be able to banish my grief? I wished I could talk to Marc about it; he always had such a clear head about problems. But Marc was gone; in fact, if Marc were here, I never would have come up with the Destiny Club in the first place.

Hally, lying next to me on the bed, sensed my distress. She raised her little head, gazed at me curiously for a few seconds, then snuggled more tightly against me. It was as if she was trying to comfort me in the only way she knew how. I began to stroke her, and when I heard her soft purring I felt some of the tension begin to leave my body. Finally I was able to compose myself enough to make the necessary calls to my part of the group, with Julie calling hers. During my brief calls, my mind was so overtaken with guilt that I found it difficult to speak.

Afterwards, in a desperate need to keep occupied, I went to the kitchen and heated water to make tea. While waiting for the tea to steep, I began thinking back through each of our histories—searching for some glimmer of a past tendency toward pathological behavior. I also needed to check the latest schedule. But then I immediately realized that the schedule wouldn't help yet. I still wouldn't be able to determine if any of us had been Destiny when this latest victim was murdered until Metro pinpointed the time when the death had actually taken place.

Thankfully, the weather was still warm enough to swim. Since swimming is one of my best stress busters, as well as helping me to clear my head, I donned my bikini and headed for my pool. I am neither a graceful swimmer nor a skillful swimmer. But my body feels good in the water. As I did my leisurely laps, I allowed my mind to go back to wondering if one of us was a serial killer. Of course I could eliminate myself. But what did I really know about my friends? What could have occurred in any of their lives during the years when we had gone our separate ways until recently, when we had regrouped again? I began going down the list in as much detail as possible of what I did know about each of them, or at least what I believed I knew.

Cassandra was the most outgoing of the group and had also been the wildest in high school. Many times back then she had enlightened our limited sexual knowledge by relating her adventures. She seemed to have a propensity for older guys, who taught her things certainly none of the rest of us had experienced. She was an only child, with doting, loving, permissive parents, and had not wanted for anything while growing up. I didn't know much of her history after we all had gone our separate ways after high school graduation, other than she had lived in California and done some modeling, even appearing in a few television commercials. She had been married four times, thrice divorced and once widowed. As far as I knew she was happy with her new single status, and had come out financially well from her divorce. Actually, she had done well financially from all four of her previous husbands. As far as outward appearances went, Cassandra was gregarious and enjoyed life.

She had been quite young when she married the first time, and had one child, a daughter, from that marriage. She also had another daughter from her second marriage, but no children from her third marriage, which was when she had been widowed, and no children from her fourth. She seemed devoted to her two children, who resided in California. I wasn't sure how her third husband had died and decided it might be important for me to find out. Did she harbor some secret, seething hatred against men from something that had happened to her in her past?

Next was Nikki, who was one of the more sensible women in the group. She had two sisters and a brother, and had come from a loving family. Her siblings were now scattered in different locations, with none presently living in Las Vegas; but as far as I knew, they were all still emotionally close. She was one of the two in our group still on her first marriage, which to all appearances was very happy. She had two grown children.

Third was Amber. Although she had a casual, outgoing demeanor, she was thoughtful about issues before voicing an opinion. She was on her second marriage, and appeared to be happy. However her husband did travel frequently, for days at a time, and her two sons were away at colleges in the East. I sensed that she was sometimes lonely, or maybe it was just my imagination and she was merely pensive. Now that I thought about it more in-depth, it was hard for me to discern which.

Continuing down the Destiny list, after Amber was Tiffani. If I could look like any of my friends, Tiff is the one I would choose. She seemed to have a smoldering depth, and I wondered if it was just from the color and shape of her eyes, or if she had some kind of deep desires that she kept hidden. She was on her third marriage, and she had no children. Even though her husband also traveled a good deal, she never appeared to be lonely. Maybe they had an open marriage, I speculated. Did Tiffani already have a secret life before Destiny? I realized I didn't know much about the Tiffani in the present, or actually, much about any of my friends in the present.

Next was Deena. Deena was in her second marriage and had a son and a daughter, both in private high schools. Her son was in a military school in Boston, and her daughter in a school in Switzerland. Deena was probably the wealthiest of all of us. Her husband had inherited a family investment business, which was very successful. She was some-times the most skeptical of the group, but also the first to admit when she was wrong. As far as I knew, she and her husband had a fulfilling relationship. He didn't have to travel with his work, but was an avid golfer, and frequently attended golf tournaments, often as one of the participants. Deena, on the other hand, was not a golfer. Now I was wondering if golf had caused a rift in their relationship. Again, I was merely speculating, with nothing to back up my speculation.

And then there was newlywed Kayla. Somehow I just could not imagine Kayla being anything but sweet, even though she had not had it easy during her first two marriages. Like Cassandra, Kayla had also married young the first time, and had children right away: twins, a boy and a girl. She was the only one of us who was already a young grandmother, with twin granddaughters from her daughter, who had also married young. I had heard a rumor that at one time Kayla's first husband had abused her, both physically and emotionally. But that was purely a rumor. Kayla had never mentioned being abused. She laughed easily and readily, and was devoted to her children and granddaughters. I would just about bet everything I had that she and Larry really *were* "deliriously" happy. Even if it were true that she had been abused by a past husband, it certainly didn't mean that she had developed some kind of psychic flaw compelling her to "off" men in order to avenge her abuse.

Following Kayla was Chloe; Chloe, like Nikki, was also still on her first marriage. Chloe and her husband had met while attending college and married before graduation. Chloe's husband was also still a hunk, even after so many years. They made a very attractive couple. And in the romance department, they were probably second only to Kayla and Larry. They had a grown son and daughter, both living in California. If you were to see a picture on a Christmas card of an ideal family, it would be Chloe's.

Last was Julie. Julie was the one who had been there the most for me after I had lost Marc. She was the one who had insisted that I get up, eat, get dressed, put on makeup, do my hair, and go out—even if only to a movie, or to lunch. She had held me when I cried. She had even held my hair out of the way when I had tried to drown my misery with too much wine and ended up kneeling on the floor and heaving relentlessly into a commode in one of the ladies rooms at the Mirage. Julie was in her second marriage, which, sadly, I knew was a marriage of many unhappy years. Her husband had also inherited millions from a family business that ran quite well without his input; therefore he drank and hunted animals for sport. Julie was irked by his pastimes, and they mostly lived as ships passing in the night.

However, to my knowledge, Julie did not have a boyfriend. Or if she did, she was very discreet. She had two daughters from her first marriage at a young age. One daughter was engaged to a Naval officer and lived in Hawaii, while the other daughter was in a design school in New York. Julie was always busy doing something, usually in an altruistic way. I just could not imagine Julie murdering any man, including her husband.

I was back to square one, or rather still at square one, which made me begin to wonder if I, too, would end up as one of Destiny's victims. I wondered if my spirit would be destroyed by the guilt and suspicion I was feeling. I was so torn. . . . *Should I go to the police and tell them about our club and take the chance that it would become public? That could feasibly end up causing heartache for all of us, perhaps unnecessarily, and that heartache would be my fault! Or should I just keep my mouth shut and hope that either the murders stop or someone is arrested? But if one of us is the serial killer, my concealing facts might result in more murders. And for that I would never be able to forgive myself! Besides, concealing facts relating to murder would also make me an accessory.* What a dilemma! At times like this I needed Marc so much it was nearly unbearable. I needed his wisdom. I needed to be able to talk to him about this huge problem I was facing. But then, again, if he were here, I wouldn't be facing the problem in the first place.

The days were shorter now, and when the afternoon sun began dropping behind the mountains in late afternoon, the pool water quickly became chilly. It was time for me to get out of the pool and take a hot shower. After I had showered and dried my hair, I put on my comfy robe and brewed another cup of tea. I sat down on the couch and put my feet up on an ottoman. As I sipped my tea, I tried to rationally contemplate what I should do. In an attempt to try to get a clearer picture, as I often did when faced with a problem since losing Marc, I pretended to be talking to him with my thoughts. I would think the words I wanted to say to him, and then imagine how he would answer. I had lost count of the number of times in the past year I had done this when faced with what I considered to be crossroads crises. I had found it a great help in trying to figure out which metaphoric road I should take. It helped me to be able see my problem more clearly, which helped me arrive at the best solution. As I imagined what he would advise me to do, I would almost be able to hear his voice saying the words.

Unfortunately, this time it didn't work. I wished I could talk it over with one of my friends. But at this point, I felt that I couldn't trust any of them. Not even Julie. If one of us had committed the murders, it could even be her! I could not absolutely rule her out! She could even be trying to throw me off her trail by calling me this morning to alert me of the discovery of the latest victim. I hadn't asked her what she was doing up so early. I groaned and shook my head as I was suddenly overcome with the harsh reality that I was the only one of the group that I knew for certain hadn't committed the murders.

But it just couldn't be Julie. Julie was my blood sister! In high school we had pricked our index fingers and each of us had marked one side of an "X" with our blood on a sheet of paper. We had signed our names underneath, pledging to be blood sisters forever. I finally decided that maybe I could eliminate Julie as one of the suspects. Julie was one of the sanest persons I knew . . . but then, so were the rest of the group. It just had to be some kind of terrible coincidence! And since I was responsible for this mess, I had to find the solution—one way or another! It didn't look like Metro was having much luck so far; it was becoming evident that they could use some help—even if it was clandestine help.

I realized I had just emotionally committed myself to become a reluctant, but necessary, sleuth in a serial murder case. I wouldn't be able to let any of the others know what I was doing—just in case one of them truly was, in fact, the killer. I didn't want to be putting myself in any needless danger, and I hoped that since Marc was no longer physically with me on Earth, that he had become my guardian angel and would be watching over me.

But I wasn't a Kinsey Millhone or even a Jessica Fletcher. I had no prior sleuthing experience. *Just where and how did an amateur sleuth begin an investigation?* My body was suddenly overtaken by a violent shudder, sloshing most of the tea onto my lap. I noticed my hands were shaking as I wiped up the mess. They seemed to be doing that a good deal of the time lately. I brewed another cup of tea, and as I sipped it, I studied the first Destiny schedule. Maybe it would be helpful to make a chart listing all of the Destiny dates, with the individual names alongside. Maybe being able to visualize it would make it clearer. I got a yellow legal pad and a pen. After I had completed making my chart, I made a list of the dates on which the murders had taken place and the locations where the victims had been found.

As I had already known, the night before the first victim was found, Chloe had been Destiny. But for the second murder, no one had been on the Destiny schedule, nor had anyone been on the schedule for the third murder. This last victim had been dead for at least several days, with the body partially decomposed and ravaged by animal predators before it had been discovered. I shuddered again. Metro might not even be able to pinpoint a time of death from what remains they had to work with. I wasn't sure to what degree of sophistication forensic pathology had evolved. For all I knew, they might even have to try to establish the time of death by narrowing down the last time the victim had been seen alive. I wondered just how close in factuality the popular TV series *CSI* was to our real Metro CSI.

I went over the revised Destiny schedule covering the past two weeks. In the ten days prior to the victim's remains being found, Julie, Nikki, Chloe, Deena, and I had all had a turn at being Destiny—the last having been Deena two days before. Again, the only one of us I could be positive was not the serial killer was myself. It could feasibly be Julie, Nikki, Chloe or Deena, or one of the others. Or maybe two of them were in it together, taking turns doing in the victims . . . meeting up someplace to carry it out as a duo. Not a very pleasant thought! What should I do, I wondered? How could I find out?

My heart ached. I would have to try to figure it out somehow, but I didn't have so much as a clue of a viable plan at present. I couldn't brilliantly deduce, then assemble everyone at my house like Nero Wolfe and subject them to point-blank questioning until the serial killer's identity was dramatically revealed! No, like Poirot, I would have to use my little grey cells—if I had any little grey cells left, and if I did, if I could get them to cooperate! I knew I would be living under a very unpleasant black cloud until the murders were solved. I also knew that a part of me didn't want them solved—fearing that one (or perhaps more than one?) of my oldest and dearest friends was a serial killer. How would I handle that? How would the rest of us handle that? Just thinking about it made my stomach queasy and gave me goose bumps.

Two days later we all met for lunch again, this time at Crave in Downtown Summerlin. I got there early, wanting to be first so I could study the others as they arrived. I quickly observed that distrust and worry were taking its toll on all of us; some had circles under their eyes that even concealer was unable to camouflage. Apparently I was not the only one who had been having difficulty sleeping. We were all subdued, barely speaking. I guess none of us knew exactly what to say. I also noted that we were guardedly eyeing one another. Probably each of us was suspicious of all the others. The usual jubilance we had always experienced when we were together was starkly missing. Would we be able to get through this unscathed? I was suddenly inundated with such extreme sadness at what this was doing to us that I nearly burst into tears, and I wondered if our friendship could survive this ordeal intact.

It was obvious that this thing would have to be remedied very quickly if our group relationship was ever to return to the easygoing, trusting rapport we had taken for granted for so many years. Suddenly the dam burst and I felt tears begin to cascade down my face. With my head down, I quickly excused myself with an invented urgent journey to the powder room. I felt so helpless . . . and so guilty!

After I had regained control of my emotions, I returned to the table. We more or less picked at our entrees, and within twenty minutes after our food had been served the group had dwindled by several. No one mentioned dessert, which had always been the crowning glory of our gatherings; of course no one mentioned meeting again next week, or at any other time in the future. Eventually, only Julie, Nikki and I were left. But I was still at a loss for words. For all I knew, Julie and Nikki could be a serial-killer duo! I couldn't bear that thought. I felt like I was suffocating and needed to get out of there. I quickly pleaded another appointment. Stammering in my haste, I ended up giving a self-consciously, overly-detailed apology for leaving. In the past, no elaborate excuse would have been necessary.

As I walked to the parking lot, tears were again streaming down my face. I looked skyward and said a silent prayer pleading for help, ending with a whispered: "Marc, please, I need you more than ever."

A few people standing nearby stared, but no one bothered to ask if I was all right. After all, this was Las Vegas, a place where one could see most anything and everything, even in the upscale area of Summerlin. They probably thought I had gambled away my monthly mortgage money—or worse.

As I drove home, random thoughts tumbled through my mind. Some I didn't want to grab hold of; they were too painful. I allowed them to continue to tumble—much like laundry in a dryer. As soon as I had put my car in the garage, I hurried to my bedroom, stripping off my clothes on the way. I was too exhausted to swim, so I turned on the faucets in my large tub and adjusted the water to a soothing warm temperature. As soon as it reached an appropriate level for soaking, I climbed in, immersing myself in the warm, lavender-scented water until I felt my muscles begin to relax. When my skin began to prune, I climbed out, quickly dried myself, then slipped naked into my soft, comforting bed. I took two aspirin, intending to float peacefully off to the land of Morpheus, dreaming sweet dreams of Marc.

But my mind wouldn't allow me the luxury of letting go, even in sleep. It continued to nag my guilt with one of the worst nightmares I could ever remember having since childhood: I was running down a dark alley in a location that was unfamiliar—as near as I could tell an industrial area near the freeway. It was very dark—probably in the wee hours of the morning, as there was limited traffic. I was being pursued by eight women dressed as Destiny; some had guns, some had knives, some had clubs. They were all chanting: "It's your fault! You made us into serial killers!" I was running as fast as I could and kept stumbling over dead bodies. My breath was coming in ragged gasps, burning my throat and chest. Someone began shooting at me, and just when I thought I couldn't run anymore, I began yelling: "Marc, help me! Where are you, Marc! Help me!" Thankfully, my yelling woke me up.

CHAPTER 9

——— • • • ———

I WAS DRENCHED with sweat and still gasping for breath. When I looked at the clock, I saw that I had only slept for several hours. With a pounding heart I stumbled to the bathroom, ducked under the shower and blasted myself with the cold spray. After I had cooled off and calmed down, I realized that the intensity of my remorsefulness was causing me to wallow in self-pity, which was not a help to any of us. That is when I knew I had to take some kind of immediate, positive action . . . but what?

While drying my hair, I considered various options. When I finished with my hair, I made a grilled cheese sandwich. I continued thinking as I munched, and finally decided on my plan of action. I didn't know if it was a good plan, but it seemed the most optimal of my limited choices. I slipped into a tailored suit and pulled my hair back into a French twist. I exchanged my contact lenses for eyeglasses—which I thought would more aptly fit my attempt to convey a scholarly appearance. My plan consisted of canvassing the various Strip casino bars on my own to try to find out whatever I could about the victims. Some of the earlier newspaper articles had mentioned the names of the casinos where the victims had last been seen on the nights they were murdered.

I made my list of the mentioned casinos, and I hastily devised what I thought to be a convincing cover story as I drove. At my first stop, I began making the rounds of the casino's individual watering holes, questioning the bar personnel. Eventually I got lucky and found a bartender who remembered seeing the first victim on the night he was murdered. I tried to look professional as I explained that I was a graduate student at UNLV doing research on serial killers for my doctoral dissertation in social psychology. As it turned out, I don't think it would have mattered what excuse I had used.

He was eager to talk. It was also apparent that he had already related the story to his friends and family a number of times, most likely embellishing with each telling. He spoke with great animation:

"Yeah, the guy was really smitten—can't say as I blame him! She was a real fox! He was a well-dressed high roller dude, and she zoomed in on him pretty fast. At first I thought maybe she was a high-class hooker. But then she didn't seem to be in any hurry trying to hustle the guy . . . it was more like she was just having a good time with him.

"They became cozy—if you know what I mean—and the next thing I knew they had disappeared, most likely to whoever's pad was closest—if you get my drift." He gave me a suggestive smile to illustrate his point. "Funny thing though, they were back again quite a bit later, only she'd changed her clothes. Earlier she had on a form-fitting red pantsuit in some kind of satiny material. But this time she had on a black lace dress that left nothing to the imagination; it looked expensive—maybe like a Versace or something. But they weren't here long. This time I watched them leave, and they seemed like they were in a real hurry! Clearly hot to trot! I guess he didn't get enough of her the first time around." He snickered as he raised his eyebrows.

I was barely able to stifle my excitement that maybe I had uncovered a lead, and I continued my questioning in what I hoped was a detached and professional way.

"You didn't happen to catch her name, did you? Perhaps I could interview her," I said, as my heart began to beat faster in anticipation.

"No, sorry, I didn't. But if she comes in again I'll try to get it for you." He smacked his lips together, and smiled . . . actually it was more of a leer than a smile.

I started to leave, then asked: "Are you sure it was the same woman he was with both times?"

"Oh, yeah, I'm positive! She's not one I would forget. She had this long, curly red hair, kind of messy—you know, what they call 'bed hair'?—Like she had just finished making love. . . . Say, you don't think she was the one who offed him, do you?"

I tried to hide my unease by keeping what I hoped was a bland expression on my face, and I gave him a noncommittal shrug in answer to his question.

"The cops wanted to know about her, too, and told me if I saw her in here again to give them a call. They didn't mention anything about her being a suspect, just that she could be a person of interest. Wait, I almost forgot. The detective gave me his card. I have his name and phone number right here," and he began digging around in a drawer under the counter behind the bar. "Here it is," he said, pulling out the business card.

He squinted as he began to read: "Lieutenant Norman. Yeah. He could probably give you lots of information on serial killers."

"Thanks," I said, pretending it was important and writing down the name and phone number, when in fact, Lieutenant Norman was the absolute last person I wanted to see! I tried to swallow the lump in my throat. It was obvious the bartender was describing Destiny . . . but which Destiny? The nights before the second and third victims had been found none of us had been on the Destiny schedule.

"It is interesting about the woman. Too bad you didn't get her name," I said, secretly crossing the fingers of my left hand and hoping that Metro didn't have her name yet either.

At my next stop I wasn't as lucky in finding out anything useful about the second murder. The bartender who had been on duty that night who might have remembered something was on vacation, not slated to be back for six more days.

At my third stop I totally struck out. I was unable to find anyone who remembered seeing either the third victim or anyone matching Destiny's description on the night of the murder.

However, at my last stop, for the fourth and most recent murder, I found a cocktail waitress who not only remembered the victim, but also remembered seeing him with a woman matching Destiny's description! The only problem, she couldn't remember how many nights it was before the body was found.

"Sorry, we've been very busy—several conventions in town," she explained. "One night is just like the next."

I was disappointed. For all of my "sleuthing," I still wasn't any closer to a solution than before. If anything, my interviews only served to emphasize Destiny's apparent ubiquity with the victims.

By now it was starting to get late, so I decided to go home and sleep on it. The next morning when I woke up, I still wasn't sure what to do, so I started another one of my silent, mental conversations with Marc. I hoped this time it would prove to be a help, because I had never faced a crisis quite this urgent! Thankfully, this time it did.

The answer I came up with seemed to be the only way I would be able to absolve us. We would have to resume the Destiny Club; however this time, I would secretly follow each one who was Destiny on a given night. That way, if there were to be another murder, I would know for sure if one of us was the killer. If it was one of us, perhaps I could even do something to prevent another murder. And even though it would be painfully difficult, I could make sure Lieutenant Norman received the information—anonymously of course—to make the arrest.

I wrote down my idea on a yellow legal tablet, adding details as I worked them out. As soon as I felt I had covered everything, I called Julie. Although I felt disloyal and guilty lying to her, I felt I had no choice. I had to do this strictly on my own now.

When she answered, I began my carefully planned dialogue: "Julie, I think we're in the clear. I'm pretty sure it's a coincidence about a woman matching Destiny's description being linked to the murders. I talked to a couple of the bartenders who remembered seeing the victims with someone who looks like our Destiny, but they told me they had also seen other women with the victims." I paused for a few seconds before continuing, praying she would believe my fabrication. "That information wasn't in the newspapers or on the TV news. Besides, the bodies were each found in a different area, and it would take considerable strength to move a body—especially all the way to Red Rock Canyon. None of us are physically strong enough to easily heft a body into a car without help, then back out of the car again—especially without being seen. So you call your half of the girls, and I'll call mine, and we'll get this thing going again." I realized I was holding my breath while I waited for her to reply.

"That's a good point, Jayne, about none of us being strong enough to move the bodies around. Also, according to the news reports, the first victim was bludgeoned to death. Surely he would have put up some kind of a struggle. And in that case, I don't see how one of us could have murdered him without also suffering some kind of obvious injury. I don't recall any of us suffering any type of wounds. . . . Okay then, if you think it's all right, I'll go ahead and make the calls."

"Thanks, Julie. Tell each of them to call me with their night's preference, and I'll make up the schedule. I guess we can meet for lunch again this week, too." When I hung up the phone, I breathed a huge sigh of relief!

CHAPTER 10

━━━━━━━━━ • • • ━━━━━━━━━

WE MET FOR lunch three days later, a much more convivial group than last time. It had been a busy three days for me. If I was going to be surreptitiously spying on my friends, I would need to disguise myself so that they wouldn't recognize me. When this ordeal would finally be over, I hoped they would never have to learn what I had done. As I looked around at the familiar, smiling faces . . . faces of friends with whom I had believed I would trust my life, I simply couldn't imagine one of them being a serial killer.

I had already gone shopping again and ended up buying three wigs. One was a stylish, red, pixie style; the second was what I considered a frumpy-styled, mousy brown color in medium length; and the third was a dark brunette, mid-shoulder, wavy style. I had also stocked up on a few new clothes from thrift stores. Even though I would try to be as unobtrusive as possible during my cloak-and-dagger forays, I certainly didn't want to be noticed and recognized because of what I was wearing. I couldn't be sure of what clothes I had worn during the times I had been with any of the group. I had also bought clothing in a style that I wouldn't ordinarily wear.

Later in the afternoon, at home, as I studied the new Destiny schedule, it looked like I would be in for an arduous two weeks. It made me tired just thinking about it. But, looking on the bright side, two weeks from now at our next luncheon, after everyone had taken a turn, hopefully the mystery would be satisfactorily solved.

That evening was Cassandra's turn. I had rented a car, a small, economy vehicle, to further lessen the risk of being recognized. I parked across the street from the apartment to wait for Cassandra to leave for her night as Destiny. I had disguised myself by wearing the frumpy, medium-length, mousy brown wig. I had added brown-rimmed eyeglasses, a sweat suit, and no makeup. I had never worn sweats outside of my house, and I never went without makeup away from home. Therefore I felt reasonably assured that if Cassandra did happen to notice me, I wouldn't be recognized. I would look like just one more of the many dowdy, compulsive gamblers addicted to video poker.

When Cassandra left the apartment in her Destiny garb, I tailed her to the Bellagio. Well, nothing like starting out at one of the best! I really hated going into the Bellagio looking the way I did. It was a matter of pride, even if no one would recognize me.

We both valet parked, and once inside I followed her at a discreet distance as she quickly made her way to one of the roulette tables. She didn't take long to home in on the most attractive high roller. She stood next to him and "accidentally" jostled him, slightly spilling her drink.

"Oh, I'm so sorry," she cooed, batting her eyes at him. "I hope I didn't spill anything on you."

It was obvious he was instantly taken with her, and soon abandoned his gambling to join her at a cozy banquette in one of the bars. Within thirty minutes they were leaving together. I followed as they walked to the elevators, but I couldn't follow them when they went up to a room. Now what? I guessed I'd have to hang around the elevators until I saw Cassandra reappear, wondering how long it would take. But that really wasn't a good idea. Lurking around doing nothing, I was sure to be noticed. The casinos have unbelievably high-tech security, and someone would soon wonder what I was doing. I decided it would be far more prudent to set up camp at a slot machine closest to the route we had taken upon entering.

Two, long, wearying hours later, and $50 poorer, I saw Cassandra heading my way with a grin on her face that wouldn't quit! Well, I was glad one of us had enjoyed herself! I hurried out the door ahead of her and had already retrieved my car before the valet brought hers. I shut off the engine and pretended to have trouble starting my car again until she was on her way. Then I tailed her as she drove back to Destiny's apartment. I parked down the street, and twenty minutes after she entered as Destiny she exited as Cassandra. At a safe distance I followed her back to her subdivision. Although it was guard gated, I was on her guest list since we were close friends.

I waited until she was inside the subdivision gates before pulling up to the guard shack. I gave him my name, and after gaining admittance to the subdivision I drove straight to Cassandra's street, arriving just as her garage door was closing. I parked my rental on the other side of the street, turned off the lights, and waited another hour to make sure she didn't leave again. Later, when I was finally able to exhaustedly slip between the crisp, cool sheets on my bed, I guiltily prayed that there had been another murder tonight with the body being found someplace away from the Strip. That would at least prove that Cassandra wasn't the serial killer, and in all likelihood would absolve all of us of the murders. But I couldn't know for sure until I had followed each of my friends on their Destiny night. I remembered to set my alarm for 6:00 a.m. so I could catch the news first thing in the morning. That was one down—actually two down (counting me), with seven to go, I mused drowsily as I drifted off to sleep.

When my alarm woke me the next morning, I immediately turned on my bedroom TV to check the news. There was no mention of another murder, which, in my mind, ruled out Cassandra as being the serial killer. I was even able to go back to sleep for several more hours. When I woke up again, I decided it was time I should get up and face the day. After brewing coffee, I sat at my kitchen table, still in my pajamas and robe, going over the previous Destiny schedule again. I had lost track now of how many times I had gone over it—trying to find some correlating pattern between the schedule and the murders. But there was none!

I was also still unable to convince myself that one of us was capable of such heinous behavior, or had a motive, or possessed the necessary strength to have carried out the murders and then move the bodies. Yet, it seemed with at least two of the murders, the victim had been connected to a woman answering Destiny's description. To my knowledge, no one outside of our group knew of Destiny. We had all sworn secrecy, and had all vowed that the club's existence had not been breached. I reached the same conclusion as I had all the other umpteen times I had studied the schedule: It just didn't make sense!

Also, for the umpteenth time, I longed for the magnificent little grey cells that Poirot possessed, or for the superior deductive skill of Nero Wolfe. Unfortunately those two geniuses were fictional detectives. I resigned myself to the fact that I would just have to spy on each Destiny, which would mean a stream of boring nights with little sleep. With that in mind, I went back to bed!

Tonight was Nikki's turn as Destiny. I followed the same procedure, wearing the same disguise I had used the previous night with Cassandra, except I wore a fresh set of sweats. After Nikki had been in the apartment for nearly forty minutes, I began to wonder if she was going to stay there for the rest of the evening. Finally she emerged, dressed to the nines in her Destiny guise. She got in her car, and I followed her to Aria; but instead of her hanging out at a bar, she entered Bardot. Since I was hardly dressed to partake of the renowned elegance of French dining at Bardot, I had to hang around as close to the restaurant's entrance as I could without drawing undue attention to myself. *Geez*, I wondered. *How long will it take for her to eat, especially when "fine dining"?* While she was enjoying a gourmet dinner, I was feeling annoyed and uncomfortable!

One-and-a-half hours later, she emerged, played the dollar slots for a half hour, then headed to the door with me closely behind. Once outside she gave the parking valet her ticket, as did I. With any luck she would be going home, and I would be able to call it an evening. But I knew I needed to follow her to make sure.

Her car arrived first, and I began to get antsy while waiting for mine. *What if I lost her, and she was still on the prowl to some other place?*

A valet finally pulled up with my car just as Nikki was wheeling down the drive. I thrust some bills in his hand, got in and took off. I nearly lost her at the light, but then was able to catch up with her again. She definitely was not proceeding toward the apartment, or in the direction of her home. As she drove farther away from the Strip, I followed, wondering where in the heck she was headed. After we had gone several miles she pulled into Boulder Station Casino. She parked in the covered parking garage rather than using valet parking, and I did likewise. This was very strange, but then maybe this was one of the places where she particularly liked to gamble . . . or do whatever she liked to do when she was dressed as Destiny! I followed her inside, and she quickly wove her way across the gaming floor as if she knew exactly where she was going. My heartbeat quickened. Maybe she *was* meeting someone!

She ended up at one of the casino bars featuring karaoke. I took a chance that she wouldn't recognize me in my disguise and entered the bar a minute later. She was sitting near the back at a small table by herself, and I discreetly sat at the bar on the opposite side, as much in the shadows as I could manage. Thankfully, the lighting was dim.

She ordered a drink, and when it was approximately half gone, she stood up and confidently made her way to the small stage. I had nearly forgotten that when Nikki was twenty she had been first runner-up in the Miss Las Vegas pageant. Possessing a fantastic voice, she had won "best talent" with her rendition of "Over the Rainbow." We had all expected that one day we would be buying her platinum albums and saying that we knew her when; however she had given it all up for marriage and family.

But now, she was blowing everyone in the place away, once again with singing "Over the Rainbow." Her voice was as fresh and beautiful as it had been when she was twenty! When she finished, she received a standing ovation. She followed up with "Blue Moon," and continued singing various songs for the next thirty minutes, bringing down the house with each. Her music brought tears to my eyes, evoking memories of our lives in years long past; memories of how simple and easy life had been then.

While the crowd was still clamoring for more, she stopped, bid good night, and made her exit. I was still in an emotional dither, but managed to compose myself enough to remember the business at hand. Surely Nikki wasn't the serial killer. From my observances during the evening, she hadn't so much as even spoken to any men—other than male service people.

Once we were both in our automobiles, I followed her directly to the apartment. Fifteen minutes later she emerged sans her Destiny identity and drove home. I methodically followed her inside her subdivision, staying a discreet distance behind. I parked down the street from her house and waited until I was sure she was in for the night. I mentally crossed her off my list, wondering if she had done this before on her previous Destiny nights, and if she had, why she hadn't shared her experiences with us? Whatever her reasons, I promised myself her secret would remain private as long as she wanted it that way. When I arrived home, once again, I set my alarm clock for 6:00 a.m. in order to catch the morning news on TV. And again, there was no report of another serial killing in the news the following morning, which allowed me the luxury of being able to go back to sleep.

The third night was Kayla's turn. This was only her fifth time to be Destiny. I followed the same routine as the other nights, only this time I dressed up a bit more. I wore the red pixie-cut wig and applied makeup. However I included the glasses again; I felt they enhanced the disguise. I donned a semi-dressy pantsuit. That way, if Kayla ended up going into an upscale bar or restaurant, I would be able to pose as a bona fide patron, rather than having to hang around the slots outside. After going to the apartment and donning her Destiny garb, Kayla went to The Venetian. She made her way to one of the bars where she ordered a glass of wine and settled in at one of the small tables. *Perhaps we had been wrong about our sweet little newlywed. Maybe she possessed lascivious undercurrents of which we were unaware.*

But my ponderings were soon interrupted when in walked Larry, elegantly dressed. He also ordered a drink, and while glancing around the room, his eyes came to rest admiringly on Kayla. She demurely looked down into her glass of wine, then coyly moved her eyes back to his. When they made eye contact again, this time she held his gaze for several seconds before looking away. He smiled, crossed to where she was sitting and sat down. After blatant flirting on both their parts for about an hour, they left the bar and went for a romantic gondola ride. My impatience in awaiting their return was rewarded with the opportunity of watching them stroll, arm in arm, to the lobby, where they entered one of the elevators.

Obviously I couldn't follow them. But at least I felt it would be safe for me to go home now. I was certain the last thing on their agenda for the evening was to commit a quick murder. However, just for the heck of it, I waited five more minutes, picked up a house phone and asked the desk clerk to ring a room in their name. When Larry answered on the second ring, I hung up. What a nice little game they had going. What great foreplay to spice up their marriage a bit—not that their marriage probably needed any spicing up. Well, that was one husband who was very much aware of the existence of Destiny!

On my drive home, I thought of how Marc and I had done something similar several times, one of them being when we were in Paris celebrating our second anniversary. I felt myself beginning to slide back into my all too familiar depression, and I had to fight to snap myself out of it. When I got home, I followed my usual new habit of setting my alarm clock. And, again, I almost hoped that there had been another murder tonight, which would mean that we were in the clear and I could stop my nightly sleuthing. Having to dress up in a disguise every night and stay out late was beginning to wear on me, both physically and emotionally.

It took me a while to fall asleep, but when I did, I slept soundly until my alarm woke me the next morning. Once again, there had been no murders.

The next night I dutifully continued my surveillance pattern, even though my chronic night-owl carousing was beginning to take its toll. However I couldn't quit now, no matter how much I longed to be able to stay home, go to bed early for a change . . . maybe start reading a good book. I steadfastly followed the same plan as I had done the previous three nights. Tonight was Tiffani's turn; after tonight, I would be halfway through the list.

Since each night I had to follow the designated Destiny, I was never sure where I would end up. Therefore I felt it was imperative to continue doing a different disguise each time in case I would be unlucky enough to happen to be in the same casino two or more nights in a row. I didn't want any casino security guards to remember someone of my description skulking around, night after night. It would be even worse to end up in the video footage on some casino's sophisticated security cameras. I certainly didn't want to be mistaken for someone having an unsavory motive—which, in essence, I guessed I did. But that didn't mean I had to look the part!

Tonight I thought my disguise should be dowdy, but presentable. I pulled on the brunette wig and swept the hair back on each side, securing it with small combs. I topped it off by adding an ecru, straw fedora I'd had for ages, but seldom wore. None of the others had ever seen me wear it. I thought it a nice extra touch in concealing my identity. Next, I put in brown contact lenses to change the color of my eyes. Lastly, I dressed in relaxed dark blue jeans a size larger than I normally wear, a white shirt, and a light-weight, navy blue jacket a size too large. The jacket had double breasted brass buttons down the front, which gave it a little touch of class. I had picked up this newest addition to my disguise clothing wardrobe earlier in the day at a Salvation Army Thrift Store.

I was waiting, parked across the street in my rental car when Tiffani left the apartment dressed as Destiny. Stifling a yawn, I wondered if I would be in for another boring evening. I was pretty sure where she was headed, remembering that on her Destiny nights her favorite hangout was Caesars. I suddenly recalled a trick we used in high school where we would "follow" someone from in front, rather than from behind. The way it worked was to be either directly in front of, or not more than one car length in front of the car we wanted to "follow." We would watch the rearview mirror for a turn signal so we could turn onto the same street as the car in question, only we would be ahead of it, rather than behind it.

We primarily used it when we wanted to know where an errant boyfriend was going, and/or if we suspected another girl was trying to move in on one of our boyfriends. Although it could be tricky, it often worked very well if we were in a car unknown to the subject being "followed"; the subject wouldn't have any inkling that he/she was being tailed from in front. Even though there was a small chance I could lose her, I decided to use our old technique on Tiffani; the benefits outweighed the risks if I arrived first.

Just before she started her car, I was able to pull onto the street ahead of her. Sure enough, after a few minutes of "following" in front of her, we turned onto Las Vegas Boulevard, also known as the Strip. I was glad I had decided to take the chance, as it served my purpose well; it allowed me to be able to valet park and hurry in ahead of her so there could be no chance of her getting away from me.

Once inside, I quickly moved out of the way of the mob of people entering behind me. I began to forage in my purse as if intent on finding an important object until I spotted Tiffani coming through the door. I closed my purse and followed her, keeping just far enough behind for her to be unaware of me, but close enough to keep her in sight.

As it was, I didn't have far to go. She walked purposefully to Cleopatra's Barge. I lingered a moment or two before following her inside. I asked to be seated in a corner as far away from Tiffani as possible and tried to make myself nondescript. To my surprise, she was soon joined by an attractive, well-dressed man. Had my secret suspicion of Tiffani having hidden deep desires possibly been intuitive? Perhaps I *didn't* really know these women whom I considered to be my best friends after all. Maybe Tiffani was in fact the serial killer, and this man was to be her next victim!

It was apparent that Tiffani's meeting with her male "friend" had been prearranged. I ordered a glass of cabernet and continued my observance, hoping no one would notice my interest. Just when I was beginning to adjust to the fact that Tiffani was enjoying having drinks with a man who wasn't her husband . . . a man who could even conceivably be the next murder victim, her younger sister Dawn joined them. While Tiffani and her male "friend" were warmly greeting Dawn, I was nearly choking on my drink. I was having enough trouble trying to cope with the idea of Tiffani having an illicit affair—or worse. The possibility of a *ménage a trois* with her sister was too much!

With their heads bent closely together in order to hear over the amplified music, the three of them began what appeared to be an earnest discussion. This served to pique my curiosity even further. Were they working out the lurid details? Perhaps negotiating a fee for services? After approximately fifteen minutes, they transitioned into a celebratory mood, enjoying the music and a second round of drinks. When they finally rose to leave, I bent down, pretending to search for something I had dropped on the floor. I certainly didn't want to take any chances on them seeing through my tacky disguise.

I needn't have worried. They were so engrossed in conversation that they didn't even glance in my direction on their way out. I waited until they were a safe distance ahead, then got up and followed them.

Instead of going to the lobby to check into a room like I had imagined, they progressed outside, where Tiffani handed her ticket to a valet to retrieve her car.

Luckily, I was close enough behind them that I was able to hand my ticket to another valet only seconds later. However, after the valet brought Tiffani's car, I had to wait another half minute until mine arrived. Even though they had already left, on a hunch, I had no trouble picking up their trail. I wasn't terribly surprised when they drove to Destiny's apartment; why pay for a room when they could have the enjoyment of privacy at the apartment? However I was still having a problem with the concept of a threesome. I wondered how many others in our group had erotic secrets of which I was unaware? At this point, I felt terribly naïve and unworldly.

I parked across the street and settled in for my surveillance. Three hours later when a taxi pulled up, I watched the man emerge from the apartment—alone—and get in. Well, at least they hadn't murdered him, I thought in relief as the taxi drove away. Picturing them engaged in a threesome was bad enough; but for Tiffani and Dawn to also have been serial killers would have been more than I could have handled, especially in my sleep-deprived condition. Thirty minutes later, Tiffani and Dawn left in Tiffani's car. I tailed them back to Caesars, where Tiffani dropped off Dawn to get her car. Afterwards I followed Tiffani as she drove to her home. I followed her inside her subdivision, staying a discrete distance behind, and parked near her house. I waited my usual hour after she had gone inside before feeling it was safe enough for me to rule out any murders occurring tonight and leave.

Even though when I arrived home I was so tired I barely had the energy to set my alarm, shed my clothes—leaving them in a crumpled heap on the floor, and crawl into my bed, sleep wouldn't come. I finally had to resort to taking a tranquilizer. Not surprisingly, next day's newspaper and television news had no reports of another murder.

The following night I trailed Deena who was Destiny. This time I decided to have a little more glamour in my disguise. I put on a platinum blonde wig in a short, wind-blown style that I had bought when I was shopping for our Destiny wig, but never worn, and put in green contact lenses. Dark, skinny jeans, complemented by a shimmery, fitted purple top and black four-inch heels completed my ensemble.

As usual, I was parked across the street from the apartment, waiting, when Deena left as Destiny. I followed her to the Bellagio, which made me glad that I had decided to glam up my disguise a bit more tonight. Once inside, she remained near the entrance playing the slots closest to the door . . . but not for long. She was soon joined by a nice-looking man. Although I was surprised, I was not nearly as surprised as I was a few minutes later when, of all people, Amber showed up! *What was going on with my friends?* The threesome proceeded to Olives. I was sure getting tired of having to hang around the gaming floor while my friends enjoyed their evenings in the most elite of the casino restaurants. I debated about also going into Olives to have dinner. But the odds of being able to be seated anytime soon without a reservation changed my mind. Therefore, as usual, I bided my time visiting various slot and video poker machines, idly playing while watching the entrance to the restaurant, losing money while others around me hit lucrative jackpots.

Two hours later, no doubt after relishing an elegant repast, Deena, Amber, and their male "friend," emerged and headed to the Cirque du Soleil *O* theater where they went inside. Since I didn't have a ticket, I continued my vigilance outside. This plan was not going at all the way I had intended. I had no idea I would end up spending so much time hanging around casino gaming floors while my friends were engaged in the enjoyment of casino amenities!

Several times I caught myself dozing while sitting on one of the uncomfortable slot machine stools, always roused just in time by the ever-present, annoying "Wheel of Fortune" chantings. *O* seemed to last forever, but finally people started filing out and milling around the exit area. I searched for Deena and Amber. As the recessing crowd thinned to a few last-minute stragglers, there was still no sign of them. *Had I somehow missed them?* I didn't think so. *Could they still be inside?* I doubted it. I waited twenty more minutes, but no one exited or entered. *Darn! I had missed them. . . . What other explanation could there be?*

I hoofed it back to the casino entrance and went outside, still looking for them. As soon as the valet brought my car I frantically drove to the apartment. But Deena's car wasn't there. *Where could she be? Were the three of them still together . . . or, possibly, only two of them . . . ? And if this were the case, which two? Were Deena and Amber also into threesomes . . . along with Tiffani and Dawn? Or were they serial killers?* By now I was nearly in a panic! I took slow, even breaths to try to calm down and think rationally. *Maybe I was wrong about Deena and Amber, as well as being wrong about Tiffani and Dawn. There was probably a reasonable and innocent explanation for my friends' behavior tonight and the previous evening.* But the skeptical part of my mind was sarcastically screaming: *Sure!*

I continued to wait, parked across the street from the apartment, until I saw Deena's car drive up, which was another hour. I was so sleepy I felt like my eyes were burning holes through the back of my head. Twenty minutes later she left the apartment and I followed her home. By the time I set my alarm and crawled into bed, I was nearly dead on my feet.

The following day there was no mention of another murder on the news. Thank God! That night was my turn as Destiny, which I blissfully spent at home, sleeping in my comfy bed!

The next evening was Julie's turn. By this time I had come to detest my nights of intrigue. One thing this burdensome experience had taught me was that it would have been impossible for me to ever have been a successful professional private investigator. Among other things, I would never have been able to adjust to the tedium of the stakeouts. Because of this recently acquired revelation, I almost decided to blow off following Julie. Of all of us in the group, Julie was the absolute last person I would suspect of being a serial killer. But then, I had to be thorough. After all, in many of the mystery thrillers, wasn't the murderer often the very last person anyone would suspect as being capable of committing murder? That meant I couldn't leave anyone out. Not even Julie. So, as fate would have it, my compulsiveness wouldn't allow me the respite of staying home. As it was, the evening turned out to be stressful, serving only to temporarily thicken the plot.

CHAPTER 11

———— • • • ————

I KNEW I had to be particularly careful with my disguise; Julie probably knew me better than any of the others. I fell back on my super dowdy look with the sweats, frumpy hair and brown-rimmed glasses. Even if Julie should happen to glance at me and think I looked vaguely familiar in some way, she would never consider that it would be me out in public in baggy sweats with no makeup. I did almost forget to add the glasses, making it all the way to my car in the garage before I remembered.

Having to go back for my glasses caused me to reach the apartment a few minutes later than I had planned. I parked in my usual place across the street, and just as I was getting settled in for my surveillance vigil, Julie exited dressed as Destiny. I was glad I hadn't arrived any later or I would have missed her. I followed her to the Mirage, and once we had both valet parked and were inside, it didn't take long for her to reach her destination. Portofino. That was when I realized I had made the wrong choice again in my disguise. Although I had originally thought my dowdy look would be best for tonight, it turned out not to have been the wisest choice. Portofino was one of the most exclusive restaurants in Las Vegas, with an opulent menu. Naturally, dressed the way I was, I couldn't follow Julie into Portofino.

Once more, as I had been forced to do so many other times during this investigation, I ended up having to hang around playing the slots. I found some nickel machines close enough to be able to keep an eye on Portofino's entrance. I figured I had about two hours before she would be finished with her "fine dining." I resolved to make the best of my situation and ordered a glass of cabernet from one of the floating cocktail waitresses. I inserted a twenty dollar bill and started playing. Who knew? Maybe this would be the time I would get lucky and win!

Two glasses of wine and fifteen dollars ahead later, I saw Julie coming out of Portofino. But she wasn't alone. From all that had transpired the past several nights, by now I thought I would have built up an immunity to surprises. Not so! I was unable to keep my jaw from literally dropping as I watched Julie coming out of Portofino, with Nikki, and a tall, distinguished man! The man was in the middle, with one arm around Julie and his other arm around Nikki, and they were all laughing. *What was going on?* It had never entered my mind that Julie wouldn't be dining alone.

I flashed back to the time I had briefly considered—then deemed the idea absurd—the possibility of Julie and Nikki being a serial killer duo. But now I wondered. . . . Had my speculation been a burst of clairvoyance? I closed my eyes and tried to clear my mind.

When I was able to gather my wits, Julie and Nikki—still accompanied by their male friend, were a good distance ahead of me. The Mirage was having a busy night, and as I tried to follow them, weaving my way through the crowd thronging the high-stakes areas, I lost them! I couldn't believe it! They just suddenly vanished! *Where could they have gone?* I hurriedly surveyed the area where I had last glimpsed them. Then I retraced my steps; still no sign of them. *Now what?* I wondered.

I hung around the area for a while, but they failed to resurface. The only thing I could think of was to drive back to the apartment to see if they happened to show up there. But when I cruised past, neither of their cars were parked anywhere around, including in the covered parking area. Considering the possibility that they could have ridden there in their male friend's car, I parked down the street, wondering what I should do. Even though there were no lights showing through the apartment windows, I finally I got out of my car and took the chance of sneaking inside the building. I rode the elevator up and crept down the hall to the apartment door to see if I could hear anything inside. It was quiet. This only served to prove that if Julie and Nikki *were* entertaining their male friend someplace, it wasn't in Destiny's apartment.

This night had surely ended up being unsettling; all it had done was to increase the cloud of suspicion. Would the man I had seen with Julie and Nikki end up being murdered tonight?

I returned to my car and waited for another hour, just in case they showed up. When they didn't, I began to wonder if Julie was by chance already home. I drove to her house to check, which wasn't difficult because we lived in the same subdivision. The only light on at Julie's house was her porch light. Since I was still using a rental car that none of the others had seen, I parked across the street from her house to watch and wait. I marked my time by dreaming of how when I returned home I would reward myself by diving into my bed with a giant bowl of Triple-Chocolate Ice Cream. At 2:14 a.m. I watched Julie pull her Lexus into her garage. *Where on earth had she been? And had Nikki been with her all of this time? Had the man I had seen them with been murdered?*

When I awoke the next morning, I realized I had been so tired last night that I had forgotten to set my alarm. I had slept through the 6:00 a.m. news and the ensuing morning news casts. Now I would have to wait until the noon news to see if there had been another murder last night. Even though no one was on the Destiny schedule for tonight, giving me a reprieve, I found it impossible to rest. My mind kept picturing Julie—dressed as Destiny—with Nikki, and both of them laughing with an unknown man who had an arm around each of them.

When there was no mention in the noon news of a body being discovered, I breathed a sigh of relief, even though I still had unanswered questions. *Maybe Julie and Nikki were also into threesomes . . . like Deena and Amber, and Tiffani and her sister? Was everyone into threesomes now, except for me, and Kayla and Larry?* Marc and I had always had such a fulfilling physical relationship, it had never entered my mind to add another person to our love making. *Was I a total square? Was I missing out on some kind of unique, erotic ecstasy?* Somehow I doubted it. However, even with all of my misgivings about some of the secret sexual preferences my friends seemed to favor, I still breathed a little easier. I had now eliminated seven of us as the serial killer—counting myself. I was beginning to feel like we were nearly home free and that the Destiny connection the police investigation was trying to make to the murders would prove to be groundless.

Tonight was Amber's turn; tomorrow night would be Chloe's turn. I would be so glad when the next two nights were over. I was becoming unbelievably weary of this onus. Thank God I had been able to grab some sleep during the days. Without the daytime sleep, I never would have been able to have maintained the stamina required for my grueling nightly spying. I desperately needed a vacation from my nocturnal espionage.

By now, I was so into the routine that it didn't take me long to get ready for Amber's Destiny. This time I again opted for the dowdy but presentable disguise I had worn for Tiffani's night of Destiny when she had met her sister Dawn and an unknown male "friend." Only this time I left off the barrettes and fedora. I mugged at my reflection in the mirror. I was even starting to grow a bit fond of some of my other "selves," even the slattern sweats self. In a sardonic way, I found it amusing to occasionally be the antithesis of my Destiny identity.

Since I had my routine down pat now, I was parked across the street and ready when Amber exited the apartment dressed as Destiny. I had no trouble following her to the Cosmopolitan. I prepared myself for all possibilities, even though I didn't think anything could surprise me now. So I pretty much took it in stride when I followed her inside the Cosmopolitan to find Deena waiting for her. I wondered if they would be meeting the same man again. I followed them, staying a safe distance behind. They threaded their way through the mass of reveling gamblers to The Chandelier Bar. When they got on the elevator, I took the stairs to the second tier of the bar where I could watch from a safe distance to see where they would end up. They rode to the top tier, where a man was already waiting for them. However it was a different man from the one they had been with on Deena's night of Destiny. What's more, I had been wrong in my thinking that nothing could surprise me now. I was nearly bowled over to see Kayla sitting beside the man awaiting their arrival. *Could it possibly be a foursome?* I shook my head. *Of course not! These were my friends. Besides, Kayla would never cheat on Larry. They were too much in love!* Whatever Amber, Deena, Kayla, and this man were up to together, it had to be something innocent.

After Amber and Deena greeted Kayla and her gentleman friend with a warm round of hugs, it appeared they were settled in for a good while. I remained on the second tier, feeling relatively secure in my vantage point. The Chandelier's long strands of beads descending from the top tier to the bottom offered a partial concealment. Perched at a small table, I was able to maintain veiled glances at them. They seemed to be engaged in a very animated conversation. While I nursed a Verbena, one of The Chandelier Bar's signature drinks, I wondered what in the heck was going on. They clinked their glasses together several times in toasts and finished off the gathering with a bottle of champagne. *Something was definitely going on . . . but what? Would they share this experience with the rest of us at our next luncheon?*

Suddenly they all rose, as if in a hurry. Due to my surprise at their hasty departure, I was delayed with settling up my tab. By the time I exited the bar they were nowhere in sight. I fruitlessly scanned the area, walking around the gaming floor looking for them. This was three nights in a row now that I had failed in my shadowing technique by losing my quarries. Once again, not knowing what else to do, I decided to drive back to the apartment. When I did, I saw the parked cars belonging to all three of my friends, which redeemed my shadowing record somewhat by putting me back to only two losses.

I figured they must all be inside, and I wondered if their gentleman friend was also with them? I watched until I saw Kayla and Deena walking out together; they chatted briefly, before going to their respective cars. I wouldn't follow either of them, since Amber was still inside. *Would the man they had been with tonight be found murdered tomorrow? Could the three of them possibly be a serial killer team? Or maybe it was only Amber. . . . Perhaps the man was still with her and being murdered at this very moment.* I took a deep breath. My imagination was running wild again.

Within thirty minutes, Amber emerged without her Destiny garb. She was also, to my relief, not hauling along a dead body. I watched as she went to her car, and I followed her as she drove home.

I was so tired I felt like sleeping the rest of the night in my car parked down the street from Amber's house. But I knew I couldn't do that. Somehow I found the energy to drive home, stripping off my clothes and wig as I staggered to my bed.

After nine hours of sleep, the next day I felt rested and ready for Chloe's Destiny. To my relief, there was nothing in either the newspaper or television news about another murder. Only one more Destiny night to go, and my charade would be over. I was beginning to feel somewhat foolish that I had suspected my friends of being serial killers. They may be into other things—kinky things; but not murder.

That night I followed the same routine with Chloe. This time I chose the red-haired pixie-style wig, green contact lenses, and I opted for a fancy dress and heels. I was tired of being frumpy and dowdy! Besides, I wanted to be ready to go inside an upscale restaurant or bar should the need arise, rather than hanging around the slots and video poker machines.

Chloe went to Caesars, which made me doubly glad that I had chosen one of my more glamorous disguises. It didn't take her long to latch onto an extremely attractive man at one of the high-dollar blackjack tables. Approximately thirty minutes later they strolled outside, holding hands, and the three of us each retrieved our respective vehicles from valet parking. Then the three of us drove in procession, with Chloe leading in her Beemer, her attractive conquest close behind in his Mercedes, and me bringing up the rear, following from a safe distance in my rental compact. I wasn't worried about losing them, since by the route they were taking I was confident of their destination: they were heading toward Destiny's apartment. Once they were inside the apartment, I parked my trusty rental car across the street and waited.

After having witnessed the unexpectedly bizarre behavior of my friends the past week and a half, although I was surprised by Chloe's tryst, I wasn't really shocked. However, out of everyone in the group, she would be one of the last I would have suspected of cheating on her husband.

Three hours later they emerged. Following what I hoped was their last passionate kiss of the evening, they parted. He got into his car, and Chloe, still dressed as Destiny, got into hers. I prayed their rendezvous for the evening had ended. I wasn't in the mood to follow them to another location for them to continue their amorous games. I was tired and more than ready to go home. I was greedy for sleep!

As Chloe eased her Beemer away from the curb, I started my engine. Thank God her paramour for the evening began traveling in the opposite direction—most likely back to Caesars. Actually, I didn't care where he was going; I was just glad that I could go home now. When I glanced in my rearview mirror, I noticed a black Lincoln pulling out of a side street behind him, heading in his same direction; rather strange, I thought, at that time of night, for another car to be pulling onto the same street at the same time. It was not a high traffic area, especially at 1:22 a.m. *Maybe Chloe's paramour was also being tailed—perhaps by a jealous wife or lover*, I thought in ironic amusement. *No, probably just pure coincidence*, I reasoned. I nearly pulled into the next driveway on a whim to turn around and join the cortege, just to see if it really was a jealous wife. But I was much too tired for more melodrama. Besides, I needed to make sure that Chloe made it home without stopping on the way to knock someone off, and that once home, she intended to remain there for the rest of the night.

An hour-and-a-half later my bed felt like Heaven! Ah, I had finished my last night of this absurd shadowing. *No more nights of this torture*, I thought, breathing a sigh of relief. Just as I was slipping into the Land of Nod, with Hally snuggled next to me, I whispered: "Thank you, Marc, for being my guardian angel and helping to guide me through this."

I was thankful that Chloe wasn't the serial killer. I was relieved that none of my friends were serial killers! I slept peacefully through the night.

CHAPTER 12

THE NEXT MORNING I was almost back to my old, ebullient self! The sun was shining, the weather was balmy, and since swim season was rapidly coming to an end, I rewarded myself with a noon swim in my pool. Afterwards I languished in the sun on a chaise for fifteen minutes. I know the sun will turn my skin to leather, as well as give me cancer, but it just felt so warm and soothing; besides, I was well slathered with sunscreen.

After a shower, followed by a light, late lunch, I read for a while, then pampered myself with an afternoon nap. I woke up in time for the late afternoon television news. I was in the process of packing away my various disguises when I stiffened and quickly turned up the volume. Another murder had occurred last night. The body had been found shortly after daybreak in an arroyo in North Las Vegas. Well, now I was sure it wasn't one of us! Especially not Chloe!

But my optimism was short-lived. Suddenly the hairs on my arms and head were standing up, feeling charged with electricity as I thought about Julie and Nikki. *What if one or both of them had murdered the man I had seen them with and his body wasn't discovered until today?* I had no idea where Julie—and Nikki had gone, or what they had been doing during the hours between the time I had lost them in Aria and the time I had watched Julie drive into her garage. It had been a more than ample time span for them to have committed a murder and hidden the body in the arroyo.

The newscaster stated the latest victim had been a guest of Caesars. A photo of the victim appeared on the screen, and I quickly closed my eyes, fearing the worst. But seconds later I forced myself to look. The picture on the screen was not the man I had seen with Julie and Nikki. But he *was* the man who had been with Chloe last night! There was no mistake. *Only how could that be? Chloe hadn't been out of my sight from the time she left the apartment as Destiny until she returned home. And that man had definitely been alive when he and Chloe had parted.* Then I remembered that the first murder had also occurred on one of Chloe's Destiny nights. *Another coincidence? Not likely! That would be one coincidence too many!*

But I had followed Chloe home and watched her house for over an hour! She hadn't left again—at least not while I was there. In fact, there hadn't been another car on her street the whole time.

I felt physically ill. The second and third murders had occurred on nights when none of us had been scheduled for Destiny. *Had Chloe secretly been Destiny on those nights, too? And maybe even on the night of the fourth murder? Should I confront her?* The idea didn't seem very appealing. *But what choice did I have?* I contemplated how to go about it; *but if Chloe were the serial killer, what if she snapped while I was questioning her and murdered me? And if she wasn't, how could I explain why I was questioning her?* I had to figure out a way to question her without being obvious. *Good luck with that!* I thought. I also knew that when I did question her, it had to be done in a place public enough to insure my own safety, but not in a place so public that we couldn't talk intimately.

I sat for a moment, composing what I would say and gathering my courage before picking up the phone and dialing Chloe's number. Just then my phone rang, startling me as it always does when it rings right before I'm getting ready to make a call. I looked at my Caller ID. Even weirder, the caller was Chloe! *Synchronicity?*

I took a deep breath and let it ring two more times, picking up just before my machine answered.

CHAPTER 13

—————— • • • ——————

AN UNEXPLAINED FEELING in my gut made me think it best to pretend I hadn't looked at my Caller ID and didn't know who was calling. Therefore, when I answered, rather than saying her name, I merely said "Hello" with a slight question in my voice.

"Hello, Jayne," Chloe said softly. I didn't say anything, waiting for her to continue. The seconds ticked away, and I was beginning to wonder if she had hung up when she finally said, "Jayne, I really need to talk to you."

I felt my stomach tighten. *Had she heard the news? Did she want to confess that she was the serial killer . . . ? Or did she want to find out if I was on to her and then try to kill me, too?* I realized I was allowing my imagination to run amok—a common occurrence of late. *But this was Chloe, for God's sake! One of my oldest and dearest friends!*

"Sure, Chloe . . . when?"

"The sooner the better! Could you meet me for dinner?"

"Sure," I repeated again, annoyed at my redundancy. *Nothing like being a versatile conversationalist,* I thought sarcastically. "Where did you have in mind?"

"How about Brio in Tivoli Village? We both like Italian food, and the location is handy for both of us. Since it's a weekday, they shouldn't be too crowded."

"Sure," I repeated for the third time, wondering where my mind had run off to.

"OK, I'll make the reservation for seven o'clock. See you there." she said, followed by the click of her disconnecting the phone.

This meant I would have to cancel my much looked forward to restful evening at home. But I was sure that what Chloe had to tell me would prove to be much more important than whatever I would have ended up doing by myself.

All the while I was scurrying around getting ready to meet Chloe, my mind was conjuring graphic images of our meeting culminating in a gory scene rivaling those in "slasher" movies. "Get a grip!" I told myself as I backed out of my driveway in my Jaguar, the rental car still prudently hidden inside the third bay of my garage in the space I usually used for storage.

I drove to Tivoli Village and parked in the underground garage, not having any idea what to expect when I met with Chloe. But of one thing I was certain—oddities of synchronicity or coincidence be damned—my gut told me our meeting was definitely in some way related to the murders!

I couldn't shake my feelings of dread as I took the elevator up to street level and walked the short distance to Brio. Chloe was already waiting for me when I arrived. She looked as anxious as I felt. We were escorted to a booth, and we each ordered a glass of wine. The meeting suddenly felt off and awkward to me, and I was beginning to have second thoughts about being there. Since I was there at Chloe's request, I wasn't sure what to say or do. It was impossible for me to act casual and natural, like a normal evening of us meeting for dinner would have been. The air was thick with tension. While we waited for our wine, I sensed we both welcomed the delay afforded by the mundane restaurant routines. We each studied a menu, not speaking and not looking at one another until after our wine had been served and we had each ordered our entrees. I felt the ball was in her court since she had summoned me for the meeting. Besides, I didn't want to divulge what I suspected.

Chloe's voice broke the silence. "Oh, Jayne, I don't know what to do. Please forgive me for involving you, but I need your help. I don't know where else to turn! I'm so afraid, I feel like I'm going crazy!"

That's when I really looked at her. Her usual beautifully made-up, cosmetically-tanned face was the color of milk. Her blush stood out on her cheeks like red clown rouge, and she had already chewed off most of her lipstick. Her eyes were ringed with black circles, exaggerating her eyeliner and mascara, giving her almost a stereotypical Vampire effect. I had never seen her look this way, and it unnerved me even further. I was fervently beginning to wish I hadn't come and that I could suddenly invent an excuse and leave.

But I knew I couldn't. *She is Chloe,* I reminded myself, *and she chose me to be the one in which to confide her terrible secret. I can at least listen to what she wants to tell me.* I braced myself for what I was about to hear, fearing it would be a confession that she was the serial killer. *What should I do if she does confess?* I pondered. *How will I handle it?*

She cleared her throat, which abruptly snapped me out of my musings.

"I'm listening, Chloe . . . I'm here to help?" I whispered.

She was shaking, and gulped the rest of her wine, making me wish we had ordered a bottle rather than individual glasses.

"You know those murders, Jayne? Well, I was with the last victim earlier in the evening on the night he was killed. . . . And . . . that's not the worst of it. I was also with the other victims on the nights they were killed. But I didn't do it! I didn't murder any of those men! I swear!"

I exhaled the breath I had been unconsciously holding. As I searched for appropriate words, I took her hand and squeezed it, then pushed my half-full wine glass toward her. Although I needed the wine desperately, I felt she needed it more.

While she was emptying the glass, I signaled the waiter. After our glasses had once again been replenished with wine, this time from the bottle I had ordered, she continued.

"Jayne, how could it have happened? It's like I've been living in a nightmare! I didn't know where to turn or who to tell, so I just kept quiet—praying that the murders would stop or that one of the victims would be someone I hadn't been with. But that didn't happen! I knew after the second murder that it had to be more than coincidence. At one point I even began to doubt my sanity. For a short time I wondered if I *had* actually flipped out . . . if I *had* actually developed one of those other personalities during which I had committed the murders and didn't remember doing them. But then I knew that wasn't true. I remember everything that happened when I was Destiny, and I know I didn't kill anyone. But why me? Why are the men I'm with on my Destiny nights being murdered?"

She put her face in her hands and sobbed. "Oh, Jayne, I just can't stand it any longer! Tell me what I should do!"

By then she was so distraught she began to wail. I had to do something to shush her, and quickly. Even though we were in a booth, which afforded us a small amount of privacy, the way this was escalating the whole restaurant would soon end up knowing her secret. I got up and went to her. I put my arms around her and just held her and let her weep. While she sobbed, I uttered pacifying murmurs, the way I thought a mother would do with an upset toddler. I began to stroke her hair, and soon her crying subsided. She picked up her napkin and started dabbing at her tears. I returned to my side of the booth, grabbed a wad of tissues from my purse and handed them to her. After she had finished drying her eyes she gave me a weak smile. Thankfully, her crying jag had helped her regain some of her self-control.

"Thanks, Jayne. I'm sorry. I swore I wasn't going to lose it. I've just been under so much stress with this thing—you can't imagine."

She was right, I couldn't imagine. It must have been horrendous!

"When we would all meet for lunch and talk about Destiny, it was all I could do to keep from screaming. I began to dread seeing everyone. That's one of the reasons I wouldn't talk about my Destiny experiences. I was terrified! I was afraid you would all think I was the one who was murdering those men!"

"Oh, Chloe, you know we would never think that about you," I said, feeling a stab of remorse at fibbing to her, considering my own recent speculations as to her innocence.

"Thank you, Jayne. You don't know how relieved I feel to hear that."

Little did she know that this time I did know exactly how relieved she felt. I had no doubts that she was telling me the truth, and the relief that I, too, was experiencing was unbelievable.

I also knew I could never tell her, or any of the others, for that matter, of my recent Destiny surveillances. I never wanted any of them to know of my suspicions. But the mystery certainly had become more complex with Chloe's admission. Now I didn't know where to begin anew in trying to unravel this mess. If I went to the police and told them what I knew, it was pretty much a given that they would arrest Chloe. I couldn't let that happen. I had to protect her privacy, along with that of the rest of the group.

"Oh, Jayne," she interrupted my thoughts, "After that first murder, I thought it was just a strange coincidence. However to be on the safe side, for my next time to be Destiny, I did it on a different night than the night listed for me on the schedule. Then when another murder did occur to the man I had been with that night, I was in a panic! I decided I wouldn't take my turn anymore—that I would just pretend to take it. But then it became almost like a compulsion with me to see if another murder would happen. So sometimes I *would* end up taking my turns as Destiny. And each time when the man I had been with was murdered, I would feel like it was my fault—that somehow I had caused it to happen by being Destiny. But how? How could my Destiny be connected to those men being murdered? I've racked my brain trying to come up with some kind of a reason, but I can't. The only thing . . . I did lose my key to the apartment after my second or third time as Destiny. I borrowed Kayla's and had another made, but never gave it much thought . . . you don't suppose that could have anything to do with the murders, do you?"

I gave her a reassuring negative shake of my head.

"After the fourth murder, I vowed I would never be Destiny again! That from now on, whenever my turn came, I would just stay home and let the rest of you believe that I had gone ahead as usual. But then, thank God, you decided to suspend the club again, and I thought that they would stop."

"So that's the reason that you never shared details of your Destiny experiences, Chloe, like the rest of us did—because of the murders? But then you never elaborated much before the murders began, either."

"Oh, God. . . ." She put her face in her hands and began to sob again, but quietly this time. "I have another confession to make, Jayne. Please don't think I'm terrible. . . . I liked the sex. I've always liked sex—a lot! Please don't tell the others; it's too embarrassing! And John would kill me if he knew I had told anyone about his problem. You see, he's been dysfunctional—damn, I hate that word—for the past three years."

I had to admit I was surprised. I had no idea that sex was so important to Chloe. She never made racy comments, even when some of the rest of us did. She had always seemed so conservative and ladylike. I also had no idea that her husband had an erectile problem.

"John has been to several urologists, but so far none have been able to help. Of course he's tried Viagra and Cialis, and God knows anything else that he thought might help. And I keep telling him it doesn't matter, even after I discovered that it does matter. Oh, I still love him, of course, but I just can't be without sex. And Destiny gave me the perfect opportunity. It was an impersonal kind of sex; when I had sex as Destiny, it wasn't like I was really cheating on John, because, in a way, I was someone else. And I was never unfaithful to John until I was Destiny—I swear!

"Jayne, you have no idea of the fear I've been living with! Wondering if the police would arrest me. Wondering if John would find out. And the constant guilt has been insufferable! Oh, all of those poor men—and their families! Their deaths must have somehow been my fault!"

Now it was my turn to feel guilty again. *If only I hadn't come up with this idiotic idea in the first place . . . yet, at the time it had seemed such an innocuous form of fun. I couldn't help feeling responsible for Chloe's pain, as well as for the murders of five men. If I hadn't invented Destiny, none of it would have happened. Once again, the only other time I could ever remember feeling such anguish was when I had been told that Marc was dead.*

Furthermore, if the murderer wasn't caught soon, it was only a matter of time before Metro would eventually link Destiny to us. And God only knows where that would lead! The only thing that would even begin to assuage my remorse was for me to catch the killer before that happened. However, so far I certainly hadn't had much luck in that department. But until now I had been working alone. If I had help from the rest of the group. . . .

"Chloe, how would you feel if we could solve this thing ourselves without involving Metro . . . ? Find out who this serial killer is and why the murders have been connected to your Destiny?"

Her eyes fixed hopefully on mine. "Oh, Jayne? How could we do that?"

My mind was in high gear now, my imagination taking off, organizing a plan of action. I just hoped that this plan of action would be more successful than my invention of Destiny.

"Well, for starters, it would require strength from you, and it would also require involving the rest of the group. You would have to tell them what you've just told me."

Chloe looked down at her hands, which were busily shredding the wad of damp tissues she had dried her eyes with. She had been slumped down in the booth, almost as if trying to hide. But now she sat up with her back straight and looked me in the eye with determination. "OK, if that's what it takes, then I'll do it. But let's get it over with as soon as possible. I don't know how much longer I can go on with hiding this awful secret."

"Don't you worry, Chloe. We'll all support you and be there with you. The worst part of it is that you will have to be Destiny one more time."

She blinked, and her mouth quivered as she whispered, "All right, if I have to . . . just one more time."

When we were leaving, I happened to think of something. *What if it were John, Chloe's husband who was committing the murders? What if he had been secretly following Chloe when she was Destiny and killing off her conquests? Maybe she hadn't lost her key to the apartment, after all . . . maybe John had taken it. I wondered if he was presently driving a black Lincoln.* "By the way, Chloe, do you know anyone who drives a black Lincoln?"

She paused a few seconds in contemplation. "No, not that I can recall . . . why do you ask?"

"Oh, no reason. It's probably not important."

When we parted, it was nearly eight thirty, and even though it was out of my way, I decided it would be worth my while to make a stop at Caesars before going home. Perhaps I would be able to find a bartender who had been on duty last night. I might even wind up getting lucky in finding one who would remember something helpful.

I twisted my hair up again into a bun, trying to look scholarly, and donned the brown-framed glasses I now kept in my purse for quickie, emergency disguises. I used the same ruse again about writing a thesis on serial killers. On my fifth try, I hit the proverbial jackpot!

"Sure, I remember him," the bartender obliged. "Mainly because of who he was with. She was a real looker! I served them drinks right here before they moved on. But I don't remember anything unusual happening. . . . She's the one you probably need to talk to . . . she might even be listed in the phone book, or if not, maybe you could get her number through information. Her name is Destiny Aaron."

Now that shook me! I had to almost literally clamp my jaw closed with my hand to keep my mouth from flying open. It was a good thing

I wasn't taking a swallow from my drink at the time or I would have choked. *He knew Destiny's name! And if he knew her name, then Metro also most likely knew her name! But there was always the possibility that he hadn't had time yet to talk to anyone from Metro,* I thought, crossing my fingers. I dropped my pen on the floor and bent down to look for it, trying to find enough time to regain my composure. When I was once again upright on the barstool, I asked "Are you sure that was her name, Destiny Aaron?" I tried to act nonchalant, even though my stomach muscles were convulsing. "That sounds like a pretty fake name to me."

"Oh, yeah, I'm sure . . . or at least that's the name she gave me. She had on this black lace dress—really high fashion, but sexy, if you know what I mean. And she had very deep blue eyes, nearly blue violet. I hadn't ever seen that color of eyes before. She looked like someone who could be in show business, which made me think she might be someone famous. So I just came out and asked her what her name was and if she was in show business. She had one of those low, sexy voices, you know, kind of like that actress in those old black and white movies? That one named Loren something?"

I knew exactly the actress he meant. And none of us had a voice like hers. "Lauren Bacall?" I answered.

"Yeah, that's the one. Anyway, she laughed and said, 'Destiny Aaron is my name, and no, I'm not in show business.' Although that's not a name I had ever heard of, I wrote it down after she left. I wanted to make sure I wouldn't forget it just in case she really did turn out to be someone famous on the minor fringes. That Lieutenant Norman who has been around asking questions was really glad when I gave him her name. He said they'd been trying to find out who she is for months now."

My hands were shaking as I shoved some bills at him. I thanked him for his time and left, hurrying to retrieve my car from the valet. By now I was breathing hard, and not just from hurrying. Since Metro now had Destiny's name, it was only a matter of time before they tracked her to the apartment. For all I knew they already had. I wondered if anyone had checked the voicemail lately on the apartment's answering machine.

I called the apartment's phone from my cell. The machine picked up on the fourth ring, but when I attempted to access the voicemail, I got a message that my code was invalid. That was odd. I tried again, just in case I had punched in the numbers wrong. But I got the same message. As far as I knew no one had changed the retrieval code from the default number that had come with the answering machine. After one more unsuccessful try, I gave up in exasperation. I would have to check the voicemail in person.

I headed to the apartment as fast as I could, having to force myself not to exceed the legal speed limit. I didn't need the delay of a traffic ticket. Upon arrival, I looked around to make sure there were no cop cars around before entering the apartment. If there were any, they were unmarked.

There were three messages on the machine, all from Lieutenant Norman requesting Destiny to call him, leaving the same telephone number each time. Now what should I do? Should I contact him and try to explain about the Destiny Club? That was really the last thing I wanted to do at this point, especially since Chloe had been involved with the victims.

While I was at the apartment, I took the opportunity to check through the closet. But I could find nothing in Destiny's wardrobe matching the description of the black lace "Versace" dress.

CHAPTER 14

— • • • —

As soon as I walked inside my front door, I kicked off my shoes and made a beeline for the phone to call Julie. I knew it was late and she was probably asleep, but it was crucial that I talk to her. First I gave her the bad news that, if not already, Metro would soon have Destiny's address; hence the apartment was off-limits for all of us. Then I told her it was imperative for us all to meet for lunch tomorrow—that Chloe needed us like she had never needed us before. Julie was full of questions, mostly about Chloe, and tried to pump me for more information. But I told her that Chloe had to be the one to tell everyone. As usual, Julie called her half of the others and I called my half. Because the meeting was of such a private nature I had decided to host the luncheon in my home. I wanted no food servers or sommeliers hovering around who might overhear.

The next morning I was busily preparing for the luncheon when my doorbell rang. It was too early for any of the girls to be arriving, and I wasn't expecting anyone else. I peered through the peephole at a man I didn't recognize. Since I don't open the door to strangers, I silently stepped back away from the door. I had an uneasy feeling about him and started breathing faster as I waited for him to go away. I knew he wasn't a solicitor, because I lived in a guard-gated subdivision. He rang my doorbell two more times before he finally left. Twenty-five minutes later my phone rang. I listened as my machine picked up.

"Ms. Robbins, my name is Lieutenant Norman. I'm with Metro, and I need to talk to you in reference to a woman named Destiny Aaron. Please call me as soon as possible," and he left his number."

My throat constricted! *How had he connected me to Destiny?* I knew I had to talk to him right away to find out what he knew. Surely he didn't suspect *me* of being the serial killer!

My hands were shaking as I picked up the phone and dialed the number. "I need to speak to Lieutenant Norman, please," my voice squeaked.

"Lieutenant Norman, speaking."

"Yes, sir . . . this is Jayne Robbins, returning your call. You wanted to speak to me about someone named Destiny Aaron? I don't recall knowing anyone by that name," I managed to say, somehow being able to keep the trembling that I was feeling in the rest of my body from reaching my voice. I realized I was in such a panic that my teeth felt on the verge of chattering. I forced myself to slow my breathing in an effort to calm down.

"Yes, ma'am, but I think it would be better if we discussed the matter in person, rather than on the phone. Would you prefer that I come to you, or would you rather come to the station?"

Please, God, I thought, not at the station! "If you could come to my home, that would be fine. . . ." I spoke each word slowly and precisely to keep from stammering. I wondered if he could sense my apprehension, and I feared that somehow he could. "Sometime this morning, if that would be possible—I'm expecting guests for lunch at one thirty, so I'll be tied up this afternoon." I knew if he didn't come soon I would be in the hospital with a nervous breakdown. I wanted to get it over with!

"I can be there in twenty minutes, if that's convenient."

"Twenty minutes will be fine," I answered, "I'll be waiting."

Nineteen-and-a-half minutes later—I had been watching the clock, fiercely concentrating on trying to compose myself while awaiting his arrival—my doorbell rang. As I walked through the entry hall a good part of me was still in shock, wondering how I had been connected to Destiny. *Had the rest of the group also been connected?*

I peered through the peephole at the same man who had been standing in front of my door less than an hour ago. He was pleasant looking . . . actually somewhat handsome, and about my age. He was neatly dressed in a grey suit, a light grey shirt, and grey and blue striped tie. As soon as I opened the door he introduced himself. "Hello, I'm Lieutenant Norman," he said, showing me his badge. "Are you Jayne Robbins?"

"Yes, sir, I am. Won't you come in?" I said, gesturing towards the living room.

After we were both seated, he in an arm chair and I perched on an ottoman, I waited for him to speak first, not trusting myself to begin the conversation. I had decided to pretend that I was totally in the dark about Destiny until I learned exactly what he did know.

"Ms. Robbins, you may have read in the newspaper or learned in other media news sources that there seems to be a mysterious woman named Destiny Aaron, who is possibly linked to the recent serial killings."

I nodded, "Yes, it seems I did read something about that"—then I couldn't stop myself from nervously blurting—"But what could that possibly have to do with me?"

He eyed me thoughtfully for several seconds before replying. "Well, we've learned her identity and traced her to an apartment near the Strip, leased in her name; she also has a bank account, a debit card, and a Nevada driver license. But that's as far as we've been able to go. We can find no history—beyond a few months, no other records, and no one who knows her. One of our stumbling blocks is that the social security number listed on all of her records belongs to an Elizabeth Hollend, deceased, who at one time shared some bank accounts with you."

I drew in a breath while studying my hands clasped tightly in my lap. I answered in a halting voice: "Elizabeth Hollend was my maternal grandmother. . . .The last few years of her life she added me to her bank accounts in case she should become too incapacitated to handle her affairs."

"Do you have any idea how this woman, Destiny Aaron, could have had access to your grandmother's social security number?"

I shook my head.

"Can you think of anyone your grandmother might have known who could be this woman . . . possibly someone who was in your grandmother's employ at some time . . . ? Maybe a maid, or a caregiver?"

Again I shook my head. "Perhaps the woman you're looking for took the social security number from my grandmother's death certificate," I ventured helpfully. "Aren't they public record? I've heard of people assuming new identities by using deceased people's records. . . ." I most assuredly did not want any direct association between myself and Destiny!

"Well, I suppose that's possible. . . . Or the number may have just been accidentally transposed and recorded incorrectly and is now in one of those eternal computer glitches. Sorry to have bothered you." He rose to leave. "We have to follow up all leads, you understand, no matter how inconsequential they may appear. The sooner we find this mysterious woman and talk to her, the better. We're hoping she can shed some light on things. If you should happen to run across her or remember anything you think might be of help, please contact me immediately." He handed me his card.

"I certainly will, although it's most unlikely. I can't even think of anyone I know who looks like her," I chattily volunteered as I walked him to the front door.

He stopped, giving me a questioning look. "How do you know what she looks like?"

I stared lamely back at him, feeling the heat of "gotcha" flooding my body, causing my face to redden, I was sure. My mind groped for an explanation. *Hadn't the newspaper mentioned that she had red hair?* I crossed my fingers and prayed. "From the newspaper," I answered, in what I hoped sounded casually, matter-of-fact. "That she has red hair. I don't know anyone who has red hair."

"Oh, yes, of course; I had forgotten that they had printed that," he said, his eyes still fixed on mine.

I gave him a meek smile as I escorted him out. After I had closed the door and locked it, I drew in a deep breath and slowly exhaled. I watched him through the peephole as he walked to his unmarked car. Not until after he had driven away did I feel myself begin to relax; and then it was nearly to the point of collapse. I had come perilously close to blowing it with Lieutenant Norman!

CHAPTER 15

— • • • —

CHLOE WAS THE first of the group to arrive. From the way she looked, I could tell she needed a pre-luncheon boost of reassurance. Although she didn't look as bad as when I had met with her last night, she was still far from looking her usual, well-put-together self. By now—after my unexpected meeting with Lieutenant Norman—I had regained some of my courage with a little help from an early start on the wine. I reasoned that since it had helped me, Chloe could use some of the same. So for starters, I poured her a glass of chardonnay, her favorite wine, before we sat down to talk.

"Oh, Jayne, what if the others don't believe that I'm innocent of the murders? What will I do? I can't go to jail, I just can't!"

"Breathe, Chloe," I said, as I took hold of one of her hands. "Just take a deep breath, then take a sip of wine, and remember that these are your best friends. Of course they will believe that you are innocent."

I crossed my fingers again, hoping that my assurance to her would turn out to be true. One could never be sure how others would react in any given situation.

Since I had put together this luncheon in a hurry, everything was relatively simple. The menu consisted of quick and easy items, thanks to a run to Trader Joe's for several kinds of salads and artisan breads, along with a couple different varieties of bread spreads. The food, along with plates, glasses, silverware, napkins, and both red and white wines, were set out on my kitchen island. I tried to make dessert special, as it always was with our luncheons, with another quick stop at our favorite

French bakery for an assortment of goodies. I was glad that I already had everything set up and ready when Chloe arrived so I could spend my time reassuring her.

Julie was the second to arrive, and although she had no idea what the crisis was, she didn't ask any questions. She just went straight to Chloe and gave her a big hug. The others arrived soon after Julie. Once everyone was assembled in my kitchen, I asked them to help themselves to wine and food and then move to the living room. Even though curiosity was very apparent on everyone's face, no one asked any questions. Once we were all seated with our plates filled with food and our glasses filled with wine, I began:

"I know you all are curious, and I'm sorry for this urgent luncheon meeting with no explanation. I appreciate all of you coming without question. Please don't judge what you are about to hear, even though I am sure some or all of you might be shocked. I had an emergency meeting with Chloe last night, at her request, and I'll let her fill you in, in her own words."

I noticed Chloe hadn't touched a bite of her food, but had finished drinking one glass of wine and already started on a second. I sure didn't envy her. I could tell she was fighting a losing battle in trying to keep back tears. She took a deep, shuddering breath, but lost her battle. Tears began to stream down her face as she began her confession of her apparent connection to the serial killings.

Everyone listened without interruption, even though facial expressions ran the gamut from curiosity, to confusion, to shock. When Chloe was finished, everyone was compassionate and accepting of her plight, offering their unequivocal support, as I had been relatively sure they would. After ample wine, followed by tears and much hugging, followed by more wine, we were probably even closer than we had been before.

The luncheon actually ended up lasting until early evening, and I was happy that it had gone the way I had hoped. After everyone had taken the time to express their sympathy and support to Chloe, we recognized the enormity of the problem we faced. In order to help her, we needed to find a way to capture the serial killer before Chloe was arrested for murder and our Destiny Club ended up being distorted and splashed across tabloid headlines. It was just the sort of decadent behavior that people who lived elsewhere might expect to happen in "Sin City." After I finished relating the details of my meeting with Lieutenant Norman, the others realized the importance of the apartment being off-limits and how close we were to our fear of exposure becoming a reality.

We needed to act fast, and I had been giving the problem careful thought since last night. I was reasonably sure that I had come up with a workable plan, which I had already briefly run by Chloe. I began to outline the details for the rest of the group.

"Being that we all agree we have to do whatever is necessary to help Chloe, I have decided that she will have to enact another night as Destiny, following her usual routine. However this time we will all be around her as backup, covertly of course, following her every move, along with those of her selected gentleman companion.

As you all know, I own a 9-mm Glock and qualified for my concealed handgun permit ten years ago while living in Texas. Although I'm aware some of the rest of you abhor guns, I feel that each of us will need some kind of weapon should it become necessary for us to have to protect ourselves. Taking all things into consideration, in reality, we will be attempting to capture the serial killer by ourselves. If any of you have access to a handgun, I advise it to be your weapon of choice. Otherwise, perhaps a stun gun, or a knife—possibly a hunting knife, or whatever else you favor that you can easily conceal. In my opinion, a baseball bat would be a bit too cumbersome!" I said facetiously, trying to add a little levity to lighten up the mood a bit. However my attempt at witticism went completely awry, when several heads earnestly nodded back in agreement.

"Since time is of the essence, we need to set it up for tomorrow night. I hope everyone is available. In the meantime, while you all are considering my idea, I'll serve dessert."

As I cleared away the luncheon dishes, they mulled over the plan. By the time I returned with a large tray of an array of French pastries, they were in unanimous agreement.

After we had worked out all the particulars, it was nearly six-thirty; but I felt it had been an afternoon well spent. I was under no illusion that it was the best scheme in the world. However it was the most efficient strategy I had been able to devise in the limited amount of time I had been allotted for devising.

Chloe was the last to leave, and just as she was ready to walk out the door I stopped her. I needed to ask her a question that I hadn't wanted to ask in front of the others. "Chloe, by chance, on one of your Destiny nights, did you give out Destiny's name to a bartender at Caesars, or anyplace else, for that matter?"

"No, of course not. I did give Destiny's name to the men I was with, but no, not to anyone else. Why do you ask?"

"Oh, no reason. I was just curious. I hope we will have all of our answers after tomorrow night."

CHAPTER 16

— • • • —

THE NEXT MORNING I was up, showered, dressed, and breakfasted by 8:30—early by my standards. It was going to be a busy day! I started off with a couple hours of practice at an indoor shooting range. Although I knew I wouldn't be able to regain my former proficiency, it was all the time I could allow. I would just have to do the best I could. I hadn't fired my Glock in over two years . . . not since before I had lost Marc. A sudden burst of melancholia hit me hard. Marc and I had gone to this shooting range every few months to practice. I didn't have to wonder what Marc would think about my plan to catch the serial killer. He would be totally against it, fearing that I would be injured or killed. "I know you don't approve, Marc, but please watch over me," I whispered softly. I had to pause from my target practice for a few moments to regain my verve.

It had taken only a few fired shots for me to discover that I had been away from the range too long. I had to get used to firing my Glock all over again. After I had practiced for an hour and a half, my shoulders and wrists were beginning to ache and I had to stop. I hoped I wouldn't have a need to actually fire my Glock tonight, but if I did, at least I was a little bit better prepared.

After I left the firing range, I stopped off at a hardware store for a roll of duct tape and heavy-duty plastic cable ties. My next stop was a visit to Target, which provided me with five pairs of small walkie-talkies, all using the same frequency; actually, they were more in the category of kids' toys, but would serve our purpose. I packed everything, along with my Glock and extra ammo, in a black tote bag, adding pepper spray as an afterthought. I hoped I hadn't forgotten anything.

We had agreed to use only four vehicles: Chloe, of course, alone in hers; I, alone in mine for extra scouting. The others were divided four in one car and three in the other, with Nikki and Deena doing the chauffeuring. We had arranged to meet in a centrally located parking lot at 7:00 p.m. As I finished getting ready, I prayed the evening would end with the serial killer safely in custody, before another murder and with our privacy intact. And although we were prepared to do battle if necessary, I still thought it was a remote possibility that any of us would encounter actual danger.

We had decided to dress in black, and when we were all assembled at our appointed meeting place I passed out the walkie-talkies. Once inside the casino we would have to be scattered in order to provide the best surveillance without being easily detected. The walkie-talkies would afford the easiest way for all of us to be in touch at once, and they would be much more efficient than trying to use our cell phones for texting. With the walkie-talkies, we would all be able to communicate with one another instantly with the press of a button. Since casino security often wore black and used something that looked similar to our walkie-talkies, hopefully we would blend in as casino personnel and not attract undue attention. Most people on Casino gaming floors were too busy, anyway, losing money and trying to cadge free drinks to observe much else going on around them.

Since I was fairly certain that the police would have Destiny's apartment building staked out, Chloe took along a lightweight hooded trench coat to wear as a makeshift disguise. Although we felt she would be reasonably safe going into the apartment, she would have to conceal her Destiny identity as best she could when coming out. If the police happened to be doing surveillance and recognize her, our plan would be irrevocably screwed!

We parked our respective vehicles across the street and half a block down from the apartment. While we waited for Chloe to reappear, I visually scoured the area for any unmarked stakeout cars. I found at least three possibles.

Chloe had done a good job of disguising herself, because when she came out, even I barely recognized her. She was halfway back to her car before I realized who she was. She had tucked all of the auburn hair around her face inside a scarf, and under her open trench coat she was wearing a mumu type dress over her Destiny garb. Although the coat hood was down, the rest of her hair was concealed inside the back of her coat. She wore dark rimmed glasses that helped hide her exotic eye makeup. She truly looked genuinely frumpy.

She started her car and drove away slowly. A block past the apartment she pulled to the curb, stopping only long enough to remove the trench coat, scarf, glasses and mumu, which she would leave in her car. Then we drove parade-style to Caesars, as that was where she had picked up her "paramour for the evening" on her past two most recent Destiny nights.

We valet parked, and after entering the casino we split off into singles and pairs. Chloe was waiting for us by the nearest bank of slot machines. As soon as she spotted us, she walked on ahead to begin her search for a suitable candidate.

Approximately thirty minutes into her cruising the high-stakes tables, she found a likely candidate for her conquest; he was tall and handsome. I prayed he wouldn't end up being the serial killer's next victim, and I vowed to make sure that he wouldn't. I glanced around to see if I could detect the others. Some I could, and some I couldn't. But then that was the way It was supposed to be.

Chloe easily struck up a conversation with him, and in less than an hour they were heading out for a tryst at the apartment. I hoped Chloe would remember to wear the trench coat again going in, this time with the hood flipped up to hide her hair!

I made my way outside and retrieved my car, as I imagined the others were also in the process of doing. There was no particular reason to hurry; we had no need to follow Chloe since we knew her destination. None of the murders had taken place until later, so I felt things would be pretty routine until after the assignation had been completed. We had told Chloe not to drag things out any longer than necessary.

By the time I arrived at the apartment there was no sign of either Chloe or her conquest. But her car was parked nearby, with a white Lexus parked directly behind it that I surmised must belong to him. I assumed they were already safely inside. Surely if the police had spotted her, they wouldn't have had enough time to already have her in custody. I settled back in the seat, trying to relax and make myself as comfortable as possible. It wasn't long before I spotted Nikki, pulling up and parking across the street. A few minutes later Deena arrived from the opposite direction and parked on my side of the street, several buildings farther down. Two of my suspected candidates for police stakeout cars were still parked where they had been earlier. Now all we had to do was wait!

I stayed busy fighting off the seductive attempts of Somnus, nearly drifting off several times. Having gotten up earlier than usual this morning, I was starting to feel the effects. Just when I was beginning to seriously wish I had included a thermos of strong, leaded coffee in my arsenal of necessities, I spotted Chloe and her conquest coming out of the apartment. Good! She had remembered to wear the coat with the hood up to cover her hair.

After a quick parting kiss they each returned to their respective vehicles. According to our plan, Deena and her passengers would follow Chloe back to the earlier parking lot meeting place, where Chloe, after changing her clothes and stashing her Destiny garb in her car, would join them. In the meantime, I would tail her conquest. Hopefully he would return to Caesars and not complicate things by going someplace else.

Nikki and her passengers would remain at the apartment for a short while to make sure we hadn't picked up a police tail. Then they would join us at Caesars, or wherever we happened to end up. Until we were able to rendezvous again, we would keep in touch by cell phone.

As we had hoped, so far Chloe's conquest was following a route back to Caesars. Ten minutes later my cell phone rang. It was Chloe, who had now joined Deena's group, checking to see if things were proceeding as expected. I confirmed that our potential destination still appeared to be Caesars.

There was no sign this time of a black Lincoln. But after we had gone two more blocks, a maroon Cadillac that was parked at the curb with its lights off began to ease onto the street between my car and Chloe's conquest's Lexus. *Coincidence? I wouldn't take any bets on it!* A tingle of excitement coursed through me; perhaps we *were* onto something! I followed the Cadillac at a heedful distance as it seemingly continued to be tailing Chloe's conquest.

It was too dark to be able to tell how many people were in the Cadillac. However since I wasn't able to discern any movement beyond the elevated headrests, I was optimistic that there was only the driver. As we proceeded towards Caesars, I debated whether to call the others to tell them of this new development, then decided to wait until I was sure . . . but sure of what? The Cadillac could turn out to have nothing to do with Destiny or the murders.

A few minutes later we were pulling into the sweeping circular drive in front of Caesars. I watched as Chloe's conquest handed his keys to a valet and strolled toward the door. I became impatient, not wanting to lose him as I waited in the valet line behind the Cadillac for its driver to follow suit. When a valet came rushing towards me, I slid from my car, tossing my keys to him as he handed me my ticket. I bounded to the entrance, nearly colliding with the person who was hurrying inside just ahead of me. But as I gawked at the reflection in the plate glass doors, there was nothing that could have prepared me for what I was seeing. It was another Destiny!

CHAPTER 17

— • • • —

IN A DAZE, I managed to retain enough of my wits to keep walking and follow her inside. She had the same hair color and style as "our" Destiny. In fact, it looked like our exact same wig! She was wearing the same type of glamorous makeup and attire, and I even managed to catch a glimpse of the same dark blue violet eyes. Once again, I rejected the possibility of this being a coincidence. She had to be doing a deliberate impersonation of our Destiny. I was also positive that she had been the driver of the Cadillac.

She seemed to be intent on following Chloe's conquest. . . . *But why? Had she also followed him to the apartment earlier? But again, why?* This was all becoming much too creepy! Trying to catch a serial killer was scary enough, but another Destiny added to the plot was a little too bizarre!

Contrary to the mounting excitement that I was feeling, Chloe's conquest didn't seem in any particular hurry as he ambled unhurriedly to a blackjack table. Funny, most men wanted to sleep after sex—in which I assumed he and Chloe had engaged. But not this guy. He seemed to be in the mood to gamble. The Destiny imposter was definitely following him, but not getting too close. Having at last progressed to a lower-paced "chase," I was finally able to catch my breath. It was also now definitely time to call the others and fill them in on this new, totally unexpected development.

I dug in my purse, pulled out my phone and dialed Deena's cell. My news update of the Destiny imposter was met with a gasp.

"Another Destiny? How can that be? What could it mean, Jayne?" Deena burst out.

"Darned if I know. But it does tend to complicate things!" I noticed my cell phone battery was dangerously low. Damn! That was one of the things I had forgotten to do, charge my battery! Talking fast, I said: "Deena, call Nikki and fill her in. I'm not sure where I'll be when you get here; I'm near the black jack tables now, but you may have to look for me. We can use the walkie-talkies again once you're here—" my phone began to beep, then went dead.

While waiting for the others to arrive, I studied the Destiny imposter. She was tall, and very slender, like a super model. She was strikingly attired in a silky mandarin-style tunic in a shade of turquoise that becomingly set off her auburn hair. The tunic was embellished with intricate lace insets and fell to several inches above her ankles. It was slit on each side to mid-thigh, and she was wearing matching leggings underneath. Over her arm was thrown a jacket in a darker shade of turquoise. She wore gold flat-heeled sandals, and carried a small matching gold shoulder bag.

Although she stayed a relatively good distance from Chloe's conquest, it wasn't long before she decided the time was right to catch his eye. He seemed surprised to see her. She beckoned to him and began to walk away. He left the blackjack table, hurrying to catch up with her—with me bringing up the rear. I wished the others would hurry up and get here! I wasn't sure where these two would end up, and I might have trouble trying to keep tabs on them by myself.

The imposter glanced back once to make sure Chloe's conquest was following. When she came to a small open bar she sat down at one of the small tables to wait for him. I faked a sudden interest in a nearby video poker machine where I could keep my eye on her and, I began to play.

He quickly joined her and she motioned for him to sit down. As soon as he did, she put her arms around him and pulled him to her.

She began to whisper in his ear. His eyes widened. Then they rose together and started walking. All the while she kept her left arm firmly around his waist and her right arm extended toward him across her abdomen with her jacket concealing her forearm and hand. Something sinister was unquestionably going on. He most certainly did not have the look of a man anticipating an encore romantic interlude in a night of carnal pleasures.

At that instant, wouldn't you know, I hit a royal flush! Great! Just what I needed: something to draw attention to myself along with slowing me down. When the machine began its irritatingly, gleeful "ching-ing," I hastily motioned to the elderly woman playing at the machine next to me. As I was quickly making my exit, I yelled to her, "Here, you take this!" Then I took off, imagining I could physically feel her astonished eyes boring into my back. Oh, well, at least something good had come *her* way this evening. For years to come she would probably be telling her cronies about the night the crazy lady at Caesars handed over her royal flush winnings to her.

I had to scramble to keep the Destiny imposter and Chloe's conquest in sight. To my surprise, they didn't head for the elevators. Instead, they stayed on a direct route to the outside doors. They exited, with me close behind, just as Deena and Nikki were making their arrival. I couldn't remember the last time I had been so happy to see someone!

I shook my head, signaling for them to pay me no recognition. But they were so busy staring at the Destiny imposter that at first they didn't see me. When they did, they realized I was already hot on the trail. But now they were unsure as to what they should do. And I didn't know what to tell them.

The imposter showed no interest in retrieving a car as she and Chloe's conquest made their way past the valets to briskly proceed along the walkway toward Las Vegas Boulevard. I trotted along behind, hoping the others would also be able to follow. I looked back once, but could see no sign of any them. I guessed that meant I was on my own, at least temporarily.

At the corner, the imposter and Chloe's conquest had to stop in order to wait for the traffic light to change. The imposter still had her arm around him with her jacket hiding her right hand. I was now certain that she had to have either a knife or a gun pressed against his side. It was obvious that he was not accompanying her voluntarily: Chloe's conquest had undeniably become the Destiny imposter's hostage!

With the changing of the light, I joined the horde of people crossing the street along with my quarry duo. I doubted that the Destiny imposter had paid any attention to me—there was no reason that she would—which meant that now I could become a bit bolder in my shadowing technique.

When they reached the Linq Casino Hotel, I was in hot pursuit. I thought perhaps she could be taking him up to a room she had reserved. God knew I couldn't lose them! But instead, they turned onto the Linq Promenade, heading down toward the High Roller. Surely she wasn't going to take him on the High Roller to do him in. This threw me off base, and I dropped back a little, wondering what I should do. What if she was taking him to a vehicle parked in the Linq's parking garage? If that were the case, I would no longer be able to follow them on foot.

I started berating myself for not having had all the bases covered. But how could I have suspected the existence of this Destiny imposter? I had done the best I could. Yet I knew if her latest victim ended up dead, I would never be able to live with myself. I was so full of self-doubt that I barely caught sight of Nikki's Land Rover cruising down Las Vegas Boulevard. I turned around and looked behind me, and there, crossing the street on foot, were the others, practically sprinting to catch up. Bless them! They had divided into two groups: one for the vehicular tailing, and the other for the footwork. Maybe we did have most of the bases covered, after all, I prayed.

Unfortunately, the Destiny imposter was not to be underestimated: she was, in all probability, the serial killer, and a pro! I still had hopes of the remote possibility she had a room reserved at the Linq, and that she would be taking him inside through one of the bars opening onto the promenade. It would be faster and easier than having to pass through a busy front lobby. And, if that were the case, I would be able to alert security. But that was not to be. When she and her hostage reached the end of the Promenade, they cut across the walk bordering the High Roller valet parking and went into the Linq's parking garage. As they wound their way up the ramp, I realized that I had probably guessed right the first time: she was most likely taking him to another vehicle. Carrying out a murder in one of the rooms would be much too messy and inconvenient, especially with having to move the body out afterwards without being seen. As far as I could imagine, that would be next to impossible!

They stopped in front of an aged, light blue van parked on the first level, halfway down the second row. I paused beside an SUV, far enough away so as not to arouse their suspicion, and pretended to fumble in my purse for a key. My heart was pounding in my ears as I watched her force her hostage in through the van's passenger side. She looked furtively around, then quickly reached inside her purse with her other hand, pulled out a syringe and plunged its contents into the side of his neck. This was one element the news had never mentioned—that the victims had been drugged. Or maybe she was doing it for the first time tonight.

I cursed softly to myself. The poor guy might already be dying from whatever she had injected him with. Taking into account that the press had never divulged specific details about the methods used for the murders, other than the first victim had been bludgeoned to death, each murder could have been committed in a different way. For all I knew, whatever had been in that syringe could have been lethal. But there was no way I could have foreseen the twists and turns the evening was taking.

I stooped below the level of the roof of the SUV I was using to block their view of me and pulled out my walkie-talkie. I called Deena, who was barely in range, and I quickly explained where I was and that I thought another murder was in the process of taking place. I asked her to call Nikki on her cell phone, since mine was dead. I also had the presence of mind to give her the license number of the blue van. But I didn't want her to call the police just yet since they would be able to trace the call back to her cell phone. I didn't want us to be linked with what was taking place unless—or until—it was absolutely necessary. There might still be a small chance that we could capture the Destiny imposter serial killer ourselves, leave her tied up in the van, and tip off the police anonymously via a public phone.

Praying that the hostage was still alive, I rose just in time to see the imposter finish positioning him in the front passenger seat of the van to look as if he were either asleep, or perhaps had over-imbibed and passed out. She started the engine, preparing to drive away. What should I do? How could I detain her long enough for the others to get here? In an effort to distract her, I began running towards her, waving my arms and screaming like a crazy person—which wasn't difficult. At this point, I was close to being a raving maniac. However, not only did she ignore my ravings, she came close to running me down in her haste to get the hell out of the garage! I threw myself onto the cement, landing hard, and was able to roll away just in time to avoid being hit!

I painfully scrambled to my feet, and, limping from a bruised knee, started trying to chase her on foot as she sped down the ramp to exit. Now I needed the police! Damn, if only my cell phone battery wasn't dead! Then I remembered my Glock. I ripped it from my bag, gripped it tightly with both of my sweaty hands and took my stance. Aiming at her back tires, I emptied the clip, nearly deafening myself. Thankfully it was a week night so there wasn't a volley of cars entering and leaving the garage. My heart sank as I watched her careen out of the garage and around the corner to the right. However within seconds, I heard the squealing of tires, followed by a crash. Perhaps my practice this morning at the shooting range hadn't been in vain. I took a deep breath; I was shaking and soaked with perspiration.

Even though I felt like my legs were beginning to buckle, somehow I was able to limp the rest of the way down the ramp and out of the garage, passing numerous people standing around gaping in horror. Even in Las Vegas it isn't every day one sees a shoot-out in the parking garage of a Strip casino. "Someone call 911!" I yelled. "Please, someone call 911!"

CHAPTER 18

— • • • —

I REACHED THE end of the garage entryway and turned the corner. There was the van, slightly crunched, a short way up the street. The Destiny imposter had sideswiped the base of one of the High Roller supports while skidding to a stop. However it wasn't a flat tire from one of my bullets that had been the cause of her sudden halt. It was Nikki's Land Rover—now also slightly crunched—blocking the way. As I limped ahead, I could see the imposter getting out of her van. I stopped and ducked down. "Deena, where are you?" I panted into my walkie-talkie.

"We're just around the corner to the South." Deena quickly answered. "Are you all right, Jayne? I tried to contact you but you didn't answer. We heard the gunshots and then the squealing tires and the crash, and we weren't sure what we should do . . ."

"I'm fine, I think, other than a badly bruised knee! I didn't hear you trying to contact me, but I've been kind of busy. I need help! Call 911, then get down here—but be careful! The Destiny imposter crashed into the base of one of the High Roller supports and into Nikki's Land Rover. We'll have to try to surround her and take her by surprise. I hope you all brought some kind of weapons!"

"We did, and we'll be there as soon as we can split up. Three of us will come in from the other way."

I kept watching—both ways—keeping an eye on the Destiny imposter while looking for Deena. Finally I spotted Deena and Kayla sneaking around the corner and they quickly joined me. Cars planning to drive into the parking garage were stopping a safe distance away, watching and waiting to see what was going on.

By now, the Destiny imposter had Nikki and the rest of the girls out of the Land Rover and was forcing them into the back of her van at gunpoint. My God, we had to do something! I tried to summon the little grey cells, but my brain felt like it had turned to mush—along with my arms and legs. I was too old for this sort of thing! Just then I heard a burst of static on my walkie-talkie, followed by Amber's hushed voice.

"Jayne, Deena, are you there?"

"Yeah, we're here—we're still trying to figure out what to do."

"Cassandra, Chloe and I are on the other side of Nikki's Land Rover, watching from behind one of the High Roller supports. That Destiny imposter is going to lock them all in the back of her van!"

"I know. I thought the darned cops would be here by now. I guess the only thing we can do is to try to rush her from both sides. Keep your walkie-talkie open, and as soon as we get close enough I'll yell 'NOW'! Don't forget to have your weapons ready," I reminded, suddenly remembering I needed to put a fresh clip in my Glock.

"OK! Will do!"

I quickly put in a fresh clip, as Deena, Kayla and I began stealthily making our way up the street. But time had run out. The imposter was getting ready to get back inside her van. I shouted "NOW" into my walkie- talkie, and we all began to run.

The imposter couldn't help but hear us. Only she must have heard my battle cry loudest coming from Amber's walkie-talkie, because she spun around toward the others. We were now coming at her from two different directions. She began to waver, not knowing which way to aim her gun. When she finally turned towards Chloe, Cassandra yanked out her weapon of choice from under her jacket. To my astonishment, it was an old fashioned bull whip.

Cassandra expertly cracked her whip across the Destiny imposter's left shoulder, causing her to let out a surprised yelp of pain and reflexively lower her gun. Next, to my amazement, Amber aimed a small revolver at the imposter, yelling at her to drop her gun. Unfortunately it turned out to be a standoff. The imposter stood still, easily moving her gun from Chloe to Cassandra to Amber. In their haste, they had made the mistake of tightening the gap and were now grouped too closely together.

However we still had the advantage, because the imposter wasn't expecting the rest of us to be coming up behind her.

"Drop your gun!" I yelled as gruffly as I was able to manage. I pulled off one shot into the ground so she would know I wasn't bluffing—spraying the area with small concrete chips. "I have you covered. It's all over!" Then I had to stop talking because my voice was beginning to quaver.

The imposter whirled, facing me, our guns aiming at each other. Cassandra took advantage of the imposter's momentary confusion and cracked her whip again, this time hitting the imposter across her right arm and knocking the gun from her hand. It skittered across the pavement, well out of her reach.

"Amber, keep her covered while I let the others out of the van, I shouted." I faced the imposter and demanded authoritatively: "Lay the van keys on the ground and carefully scoot them towards me with your foot."

She hesitated for only a few seconds, then apparently decided she had no other option. She dropped the keys to the ground, and with the toe of her sandal she shoved them within my reach. I grabbed them up and unlocked the back of the van, releasing an extremely angry group of women!

While Amber kept the imposter covered, I put my Glock safely back in my bag and removed the cable ties and duct tape. We thought with so many of us that we would have no problem shoving the imposter into the back of the van where we could contain her. However she was so desperate to get away, that even with Amber still holding a gun on her, she struggled, kicking at us and trying to squirm out of our grasp. Soon we were all panting and sweating and starting to feel the weariness of fighting with her, and I began to fear that she would be able to break away. I felt an urgency to do something—fast!

"Amber," I said in as stern a voice as I could muster, "Maybe you should go ahead and shoot her in the kneecap so that we can get her inside the van!"

Thankfully, that did the trick. The imposter went limp, as if she had given up. However, even though we were able to finally drag her inside, we stayed wary in case she was trying to trick us into overconfidence. Amber continued to hold her at gunpoint, but from a safe distance. The imposter didn't struggle as we quickly bound her hands and feet together with duct tape. Although she hadn't attempted to yell or scream at us, I didn't want to take any chances that she might start. I decided it would be prudent to also cover her mouth with the duct tape, just in case. While applying the tape across her lips, I accidentally made eye contact with her, something I had been trying to avoid. Her heavily made-up eyes bored into mine with a look of such intense hate, that if looks could kill I would have been instantly dead.

Her baleful look gave me chills and shook me emotionally, which threw me mentally off balance for a few seconds. After all, we were pretty sure she had already killed five men—that we knew of—in cold blood, and possibly a sixth with this latest victim! There could even be more that hadn't been discovered yet! For good measure, we secured the heavy-duty cable ties tightly around her duct-taped hands and feet. Maybe this was overkill. But I didn't want to leave any chance possibility of her being able to free herself.

Some of the group wanted to give her a shot of the pepper spray, too. But I was afraid it might cause her to gag and possibly vomit. Consequently, with the duct tape covering her mount, she could aspirate the vomit into her lungs. Not a good thing to have happen. I didn't want to be responsible for any more deaths! Not even the death of a probable serial killer choking on her own vomit.

After securing her, while we were in the process of shoving her farther back inside the van, I continued wonder, as I had throughout our struggles: *Where in the hell are the damn cops when you need them? Surely from all of the 911 calls they should have been here by now!* As if in instant answer to my mental question, I heard sirens. The first squad car arrived on the scene just as we finished closing the doors to the van and locking the imposter inside.

CHAPTER 19

— • • • —

IN A MATTER of minutes, we were joined by some of Metro's finest. When the first squad car arrived, I pointed to the front seat of the van and yelled for an ambulance to be summoned, praying that the imposter's captive was still alive. One of the uniformed officers ran to the van to check the victim and related that he could feel a strong, steady pulse. Within seconds, another squad car arrived, followed shortly by an ambulance. One of the paramedics did a quick evaluation of the victim, loaded him on a stretcher and started oxygen and an IV before whisking him away to the emergency room.

"All right," bellowed one of the officers, "My name is Officer Bailey, and I'm taking charge. Just what is going on here?"

I realized how bizarre the scene must be. The police, along with a number of people in cars and pedestrian bystanders, were looking around in bewilderment. I couldn't blame them, as they could have no clue as to what had actually happened. We all started talking at once, I guess out of nervousness and shock, which ended up sounding like a cacophony of nonsensical chatter. My heart suddenly began to beat faster as I had the horrible thought that they might free the Destiny imposter before knowing who she was.

Officer Bailey suddenly gave a loud whistle out of frustration, causing all of us to stop in midsentence. I held up my hand to signal silence to the others and hurried over to him. I tried to calm myself before jumping in with the beginning of a hasty explanation, knowing I would have to improvise as I talked. He was scrutinizing all us suspiciously, and I prayed that he would believe me. So far, he had no idea that the woman we had locked in the van was the probable serial killer.

"Officer Bailey, I know this must be a confusing scene. Please let me explain. You see, my friends and I believe we have captured the person who has been murdering those men. The one you have been referring to as a serial killer. She also happens to fit the description of the woman with the red hair you have been looking for as a person of interest. We have her locked inside that van," I said, pointing.

I stopped to take a breath and to try to think how much I could say without involving us any further than necessary. I can only describe the look on his face as amazed disbelief. I know that may seem both a redundant and an overly emphatic use of words; but neither word used by itself aptly fit the expression on Officer Bailey's face. He looked as if he had a sudden need to sit down. However he was able to retain his staunch air of authority and remain standing. "Call Lieutenant Norman," he commanded to his partner. "We'll wait for his instructions as to how to proceed."

He walked over to the van. "You mean to tell me that you actually have someone locked inside this van who you profess to be the serial killer? That the red-headed woman we have been looking for as a person of interest is really the serial killer? And just how could you ladies know that for a fact?"

"Well, we just do," I said, with the others nodding in agreement.

"I still don't see how you could possibly know that this person is the serial killer." he said, unlocking and opening the back of the van to see for himself.

He was stunned to see our Destiny impersonator all trussed up with duct tape and the cable ties.

"Well, you certainly did a thorough job, that's for sure," he said, looking again as if he had a need to sit down. "So, again, according to you, this is the red-haired woman we have been looking for as a person of interest? And she is, in fact, also the serial killer? I want you women to tell me just how you can be so sure? What evidence do you have? And how did you manage to get her to surrender to you so you could hold her captive? Are you aware that if you are wrong, you are all in very serious trouble? You could all be charged with assault, along with other violations!"

Just then, Officer Bailey's partner motioned for him to come to the squad car, saying that Lieutenant Norman wanted to talk to him on the phone. This was a bit of luck, as it gave me the extra time that I badly needed to try to come up with a logical story of how we had happened to capture the serial killer.

We all waited, wondering what would happen next. When Officer Bailey had finished his conversation with Lieutenant Norman, he turned to us and said, "Well, ladies, you have all now become persons of interest yourselves. You all need to come to the station and give your statements, immediately. If you won't come voluntarily, then you will have to be cuffed and forcibly taken into custody." He looked around at all of us, waiting for our replies. We unanimously agreed to cooperate. I don't know if the others were as frightened as I was; but I had a pretty good idea that they were.

While Officer Bailey kept us under watch, his partner, along with the other two uniformed officers from the second squad car, unfastened the cable ties and tore off the duct tape on the Destiny imposter's hands and feet. They also removed the duct tape from her mouth, but she made no attempt to speak. After cuffing her, they read her rights to her before loading her into the back seat of the second squad car and driving away, this time without the siren.

"OK," stated Officer Bailey, "Now that the alleged serial killer has been taken into *official* custody for questioning, as I already told you ladies, you all need to immediately come down to the station. You can either follow me now in your own vehicles, or I can make the other arrangements that I mentioned earlier. Which will it be?"

When I faced the others, they were all staring at me questioningly. As my eyes roved over each of them in search of some helpful input, I realized that they had unofficially appointed me to be the spokesperson. Although we hadn't had time yet to make up a plausible story, I was sure none of us wanted to be cuffed and taken to the station forcibly. "Of course, Officer Bailey," I said, trying to look innocent as I turned back to face him, "We will be *happy* to voluntarily follow you to the station in our own cars to give our statements." I hoped he hadn't picked up on the sarcasm in my reply.

As Officer Bailey and his partner were climbing into their squad car, I was able to have a hurried discussion with the others before getting into our own vehicles. Even with our insistence that we had just caught the serial killer who had been eluding capture for many months, understandably, the police had no validation that this was what had actually occurred. Now that we had been able to calm down a bit, we recognized that it was certainly understandable and reasonable that we all would be required to go to the station for questioning. Maybe it would end up being a simple process of us merely relating an abridged version of the capture. Actually, we were fortunate that we were allowed to drive there in our own vehicles, rather than having to be cuffed and taken to the station in squad cars; or even more embarrassing, having to ride to the station in a paddy wagon!

Nikki's Land Rover was drivable, but it would need major body work. I crowded into Deena's Mercedes for the trip. A major part of the mystery was still unsolved. None of us had any idea who this Destiny imposter was, and Chloe still had no idea how she was connected to the murders. On the ride to the station my mind was busy with more immediate critical issues, like trying to fabricate what I hoped to be a convincing explanation for an allegedly innocuous outing that had resulted in the capture of the serial killer.

Unfortunately I wasn't able to come up with anything very credible. My knee was giving me lot of pain and beginning to swell. Besides, I was too exhausted to think.

When we arrived at the station, Officer Bailey was waiting for us. He politely escorted us into a small room which reminded me of one of the interrogation rooms shown on the TV series *Law and Order*.

Once we were all seated, another man entered the room and introduced himself as Detective Samson. "Good evening, ladies. Would any of you care for water or coffee while I get your statements?" We declined his offer in unison, wanting to get this over with as quickly as possible so we could all go home. "No? Well then first of all, I need to get your names and addresses and check your IDs."

His obvious overdone politeness made me uneasy, and I wondered what he had up his sleeve. I was sure he was suspicious of us. Why wouldn't he be? When Officer Bailey had arrived on the scene it must have seemed surreal. Actually, it still seemed surreal even to me.

After he had checked our driver licenses and recorded our names and addresses, his tone became more authoritative. "Now then, whenever you're ready, I'll begin getting your statements. Who wants to start?"

When no one spoke, it appeared that I was still the unofficial spokesperson for the group, which was probably best, even though my brain still felt like it was full of mush. I began to explain in slow, carefully chosen words.

"Well, my friends and I had gone to Caesars to enjoy a nice girls' evening out . . . you know, a nice dinner together followed by a little playing of the slots and video poker? By chance, as I was playing the video poker machine, I happened to look up and see what I thought looked like the woman you had been describing in the news as a person of interest in the serial killings. She was walking nearby with a man who looked scared. It appeared that she had some kind of a weapon hidden under her jacket and that she was forcing him to accompany her against his will. I alerted my friends that a kidnapping seemed to be in progress, and we started following them. The woman, and the man who looked like he was her hostage, walked out of Caesars, crossed the street, walked down the Linq Promenade, and ended up in the Linq's parking garage. When I saw her force him into her van and inject him with something, I tried to stop her from leaving." I paused to take a breath, wondering how I would explain carrying my Glock. I didn't have a permit. I knew it would come out that someone had shot at the Destiny imposter's van. I figured I might as well tell the truth and hope for the best.

"That's when I pulled out my gun and fired it at her tires, hoping to stop her; but I wasn't successful. In the meantime, some of my friends had gotten into Nikki's Land Rover and tried to block her after she drove out of the parking garage. It all happened by chance, just one of those crazy things. . . ."

I stopped, fearing I was overstating. *Keep it simple*, I thought, warning myself. He put his hands together and pursed his lips, not speaking. I could feel my pulse in my temples. I was so tired, I was afraid I wasn't doing a very believable job with my explanation. I also couldn't get over my gut feeling that someone was outside the room watching through a two-way mirror.

Finally, after what seemed like hours, but was probably only ten or fifteen seconds, Detective Samson spoke.

"And what, at the time, made you think that the person we now have in custody was the serial killer, and what made you start watching her?"

"I told you, she looked like the woman you have been looking for."

"Ah, yes, you did say that."

He paused to look down at some notes, and his next question nearly did me in. "Let's see now, oh, yes. How did you happen to have the cable ties and duct tape with you that you used to secure her? Is that something you ordinarily carry around with you?"

It took me several seconds to reply, and then I said the first thing that popped into my head: "Um, no sir. We found the duct tape and cable ties in her van."

"What about the walkie-talkies? Officer Baily said when he arrived on the scene that some of you had walkie-talkies?"

This question was a bit easier for me to come up with an answer, because, in part, I could tell the truth: "Oh, we use those when we are in casinos so we can keep in easy contact with one another. Cell service inside casinos is sometimes iffy."

He shook his head, but didn't pursue it further. Instead, he moved on to an even more alarming question. "What I'm most interested in, Ms. Robbins, is why you were carrying a gun in your purse—without a permit to carry?"

By now I was close to tears; my nerves were shredded. I blinked, trying very hard to keep the tears back, and swallowed.

"I was carrying the gun because I lost my husband fourteen months ago and I live alone. When I go out at night, I carry it with me for protection."

I hoped I sounded convincing. He sighed. And again, he said nothing; he just sat there, looking at me, his hands in front of him with his fingertips pressed together.

"We thought we were doing a good thing in preventing what we believed would be the next serial killing. We had to act quickly, and there was no time to call Metro first. We did call you as soon as we could. That's all there was to it," I said defensively. I was becoming resentful of having to keep going over my story. The others had remained mute during my explanation. He looked at them speculatively, his eyes moving across each of their faces, one by one. "Do you all concur with Ms. Robbins' statement?"

They all nodded and murmured their agreement.

"I don't suppose any of the rest of you have anything to add?" He asked.

Again, they all shook their heads.

"No, of course you don't," he said with a tinge of cynicism.

Since none of us had anything more to reveal, there wasn't much Metro could do but to let us go. They had nothing that they could hold us on, other than my firearms violation. However we weren't so naïve as to believe they would think it normal for ordinary women to travel around in a pack, dressed in black, sporting weapons of some sort and walkie-talkies. By no means was this to be the end of it!

No doubt, they were still suspicious of the tape and cable ties—not to mention the bullwhip we happened to have with us. I wasn't sure if they believed my statement that we had found the cable ties and duct tape in the killer's van. I think they suspected that we were some kind of a cat-burglar gang, except they could find no trace of stolen goods or burglar tools and none of us had a record. I was issued citations for carrying a concealed handgun without a permit and for discharging a firearm in the city. However, to my surprise, Amber didn't receive any similar citations—because her gun turned out to be a *toy*! When I found that out I nearly choked. Tremors ran up and down my spine as I remembered how Amber had been the one to keep the evil Destiny imposter covered—using a *toy gun*! But the gun had looked so real!

At last, when all of the paperwork was finished and we were preparing to go home, Lieutenant Norman made his appearance. That was when I was sure my gut feeling had been right; that *he* was the "someone" who had been observing us through a two-way mirror during my testimony.

He was quick to single me out: "Well, fancy seeing you here, Ms. Robbins."

His eyes drilled suspiciously into mine for several seconds before he continued. He smiled, but only with his mouth, his eyes remaining stern and distrusting. "Before you ladies leave, I want to inform you that the evidence so far strongly indicates that you have, indeed, captured the alleged serial killer. Furthermore, it seems most probable that the latest potential victim, whom you rescued—and who is going to be just fine once the narcotic wears off—will be able to give his statement. If his story corroborates yours, that additional evidence should be plenty for an indictment and conviction."

He stopped talking long enough to give each of us a brief but intense scrutiny, which gave me an "uh oh" feeling. Then he gave us a sardonic grin as he dropped his bomb. "Oh, and one more thing: did you ladies know that the suspect you captured isn't a woman?"

He carefully took note of our reaction as we all stared at him in disbelief.

"Yes. It turns out that the suspect is a man who was *dressed* as a woman." Then he turned away as he said, "You ladies be careful going home now."

We were all too tired to deal with this newest disclosure tonight. We decided it would be better to meet tomorrow after we had all had a good night's sleep. We also had to try to refine our story in more detail about how we happened to be on the scene to capture the serial killer. It was only a matter of time before Metro would want to question us again. As far as they knew, they had the woman known as Destiny Aaron in custody. They had no idea, yet, that they didn't have the real Destiny Aaron.

There was also still that connection of *our* Destiny to my grandmother's Social Security number. And most importantly, we had to figure out how Chloe was connected to the serial killer. As usual, I missed Marc's helpful input, and, for the umpteenth time, wondered if he would be disappointed in me for what I had done. Again, also for the umpteenth time, none if this would have happened if he was still here with me.

Deena dropped me off at Caesars so I could pick up my car. All I wanted to do was to go home, ice my knee, take some aspirin, and go to bed. But as soon as I got in my car I was hit with a dire reality: it wouldn't be long before Metro would be able to obtain a search warrant, and cops would be all over our Destiny's apartment looking for evidence. They would naturally believe that the apartment belonged to the suspect they had in custody. Our fingerprints were all over the place, along with our personal items full of our DNA. Even though I felt I was on the brink of total exhaustion, I knew I had to go to the apartment and remove any traces of ourselves. I might already be too late!

CHAPTER 20

─────── • • • ───────

I WAS CAREFUL not to exceed the speed limit, all the while fighting against my instinct to race there as fast as possible. I badly needed coffee; but I couldn't take the time to stop for some. When I arrived at the apartment building, I didn't see any signs that Metro had been there yet. There was no yellow crime scene tape, so I hurried inside and up to the apartment. However when I rushed inside, I found where Lieutenant Norman had shoved one of his cards underneath the door.

I started in the closet first, gathering up garments and stuffing them in the large trash bags we kept stashed in the kitchen pantry. As soon as I would fill several bags, I would lug them down in the elevator to my car and put them in the trunk. Luckily, there weren't a huge amount of clothes. Next, I emptied the contents of the bathroom medicine cabinets and drawers of all the various toiletries, sweeping them into a trash bag. I did the same with the dresser drawers in the bedroom dresser and night stands. Again, luckily, there weren't many personal items.

After I had finished removing all of the personal items, I started cleaning. Since we had felt it too risky to hire a regular cleaning service, we had made it a rule to clean up after ourselves. We had also taken turns doing weekly maintenance cleaning, which now seemed to have turned out to be one of those proverbial blessings in disguise: The apartment was already basically clean, plus, I had plenty of cleaning supplies on hand! I took paper towels dampened with glass cleaner, and I wiped every knob, handle, faucet, light switch, and any place else I could think of where there could be a fingerprint. I even did a quick scrub to the front of all of the cabinets and doors and wiped down the front of the toilet tanks and handles. For good measure, I poured some bleach in the toilet bowls and cleaned them with the brush, in case they would be checked for DNA.

Lastly, I did a quick vacuuming of the floors and upholstery with the stick vacuum cleaner we kept there. When I left, I locked the door behind me, and made sure to wipe down the outside of the door as well as the knob. As I was cramming the last of the bags and the vacuum cleaner in my car, I remembered the combination phone/answering machine. Geez, I couldn't believe I had almost forgotten to take it. I ran back up to the apartment and yanked out the plug. I did another hasty rubdown of the door knobs, this time using the edge of my jacket. I hurried back down to my car with the phone/answering machine, fervently hoping I hadn't forgotten anything else. As I was driving away, a car drove up and parked in front of the apartment; I stopped down the street and watched as two men got out and went inside the building. I was sure they were detectives. I had gotten rid of our personal belongings just in time!

I had to sit in my car for a few minutes to catch my breath. My hands were so sweaty and shaky I didn't think I would be able to drive yet. What a close call we had, hopefully, averted! If Metro had gotten to the apartment before I had, we all would have been in deep trouble. It made me shiver to think what might have happened.

When I felt calm enough to drive, I headed for home. It was probably a good thing that due to my recent exertion my knee was now throbbing with pain; otherwise I probably would have nodded off on the way. I decided I wouldn't worry about unpacking the car until tomorrow. In the meantime, it would be securely locked away in my garage. Although I felt grimy, I was too exhausted for a shower. Once home, I staggered to my bedroom, grabbing a bag of peas from the freezer for my knee on the way. I pulled off my clothes and crawled into bed naked, making a promise to myself that I would put fresh sheets on the bed in the morning. I was asleep the second my head was on the pillow.

CHAPTER 21

— • • • —

THE RINGING WAS irritating! But I couldn't find the source to make it stop. I was stumbling around in a mist so thick I was unable to see. I opened my eyes and the mist cleared, replaced by the bright cheerfulness of my bedroom. The irritating ringing was coming from my bedside phone, which stopped when the answering machine in the kitchen picked up. I groaned. My eyes felt grainy. Who the hell is calling me now, I thought. I looked at the Caller ID. It was Chloe. I picked up the phone as she was completing her message.

"Yeah, Chloe, I'm here. What's up?" I mumbled, still not fully alert.

"I'm sorry to wake you, Jayne, but I thought you should be the first to know. I was having trouble sleeping early this morning and thought maybe a cup of cocoa might help to relax me. I got up, and while I was in the kitchen, I turned on the TV . . . and there it was on the news—about the serial killer being arrested. They showed a picture of us taken at the scene! But, thankfully, they didn't give any of our names. They were telling how we helped in the capture, which was shocking enough . . . but then, when they showed the killer's face without the Destiny disguise . . . Jayne, I recognized him! He was one of my dates in the beginning of the Destiny Club. I think it was my second, or maybe my third time as Destiny that I met him and had sex with him. In fact, I went out with him more than once. He was good at it—if you know what I mean. But I stopped seeing him when he began demanding an exclusive relationship and insisting on knowing more about me. He was also beginning to hint at wanting kinky sex.

"He persisted in pursuing me until he intimidated me into giving him my phone number, which was not my home number, but the one for the apartment phone. Of course he never knew my real name. He only knew me as Destiny Aaron. He started leaving threatening voice mail on the apartment's answering machine. I had to change the retrieval code so I could intercept his messages and erase them before the rest of you found out. Jayne, I know I should have told you, but I was afraid that you would put an end to the club. And, at the time, I was enjoying it too much. Finally I told him if he didn't stop harassing me that I'd call the police. Of course he had no idea I would never be able to do that for fear of revealing our Destiny charade. But the warning was enough to end his pursuit, or so I had believed. I never once thought about him being the serial killer."

I was sitting up in bed, now wide-awake, mulling over what Chloe was telling me.

"He must have been stalking you, Chloe, whenever you were Destiny. But it surely wouldn't have taken long for him to discover that there was more than one Destiny . . . I wonder how he was able to single out your Destiny from the rest of us?

"Well, he knew my car; maybe that's how he recognized me."

"Chloe, of course! He must have staked out the apartment every night watching for your car, and on those nights when you were Destiny he would follow you. Later, he would dress in his version of Destiny and find a way to seek out the man you had been with earlier in the evening and take him hostage. Then he would forcibly take him someplace where they would be alone and kill him. What a psycho!"

"My God, Jayne, I *am* responsible for the deaths of those poor men! How will I ever be able to get through this?"

"No, Chloe, we're all equally responsible. In fact, if anything, I'm the one with the most blame. Don't forget, the Destiny Club was my idea in the first place."

Chloe and I were both crying when I hung up the phone. I immediately got up and threw on some clothes, got in the rental car and went out and bought a burner phone. I made calls to terminate the utilities and cable service at the apartment. Afterwards, to be super safe, I wiped the burner phone clean, went into a Starbuck's and bought a latte. Before leaving, I ditched the phone in the ladies room trash under a bunch of paper towels. As for our apartment lease—well, we would just have to walk away from it and lose the deposit and advance month's rent. I turned in the rental car and took a cab home.

My Jaguar was still loaded with the clothing and personal items I had removed from the apartment. After icing my knee, which thankfully was somewhat better today, I drove all the way to Boulder City, where I dropped off all of the bags of clothing at a Salvation Army location. Then I drove around until I found a large, industrial-size dumpster, where I unloaded the bags containing the cosmetics and miscellaneous items.

Later, when I drove by the apartment, there was a Crime Scene Investigation van parked outside. Once again, I hoped I had wiped out all traces of our DNA and fingerprints. I was sure they were going over the apartment with a fine-tooth comb. I didn't think they could trace any of the furnishings to us, as many were cast-offs that we'd had for years; while others had been purchased at thrift stores with cash. I felt a sudden chill run up my spine, causing me to shiver when I thought of what might have happened if I hadn't been compelled to go to the apartment last night and do what I had done. I wondered what had made me think of doing it: perhaps, it had been Marc, watching over me? I still felt he had become my guardian angel. Lord knows I needed one!

CHAPTER 22

— • • • —

WE ENDED UP meeting that evening at Kayla's home. At first we were like a bunch of magpies, all talking at once. I guess it must have been some kind of post-traumatic stress reaction. As soon as we all quieted down a bit, I scolded Amber for bringing along the toy gun as a so-called weapon. I still shuddered every time I thought about it!

"My God, Amber, you could have gotten us all killed. What were you thinking? You could at least have let me know it wasn't a real gun!"

"Sure, Jayne, and just when should have I done that? When I was holding the killer at bay while you were letting the others out of the van . . . ? Or, better yet, while you were taping his hands and feet together and securing them with the cable ties? I hardly think either of those was an appropriate time to say, 'Oh, by the way, you all, this isn't a real gun.' Besides, it fooled everyone, didn't it?"

What she said was true. I smiled. "I'm sorry, Amber. You're right, of course. But if ever there should be a next time—God forbid—please bring a real gun! Or don't bring one at all!"

And Cassandra! She had stunned all of us with her skillful bull whip artistry. When we questioned her about it, she admitted that an old boyfriend, who had been into sadomasochism, had taught her the ways of a dominatrix, including "whip arts."

After that we had talked nonstop—fortified by our unanimously favorite wine for our special get-togethers: New Age, with fresh squeezed lime. And pizza! Lots of pizza! Pizza was our favorite comfort food, and we had several different varieties. We even had one with brie, mushrooms, and truffle oil, which happened to be my personal favorite.

We ate, drank and talked until we were finally able to experience some sort of cathartic release. It was unequivocally agreed that the Destiny Club would be instantly disbanded. We also decided that the club would always be our secret. That was when Kayla shyly confessed that she had told Larry about our club, but vowed she had sworn him to secrecy. Although I was already aware of this, I did not reveal my prior knowledge to the others. However, I couldn't help smiling as I remembered their little role-playing game I had witnessed while carrying out my undercover shadowing. Of course I would keep that little romantic interlude forever secret, both for their sake, as well as for mine.

After Kayla's admission, Tiffani startled the others with her announcement that she had also breached Destiny's secret. "But it wasn't intentional," she said apologetically. "One evening I just happened to strike up a conversation with an agent who specializes in representing singers. As luck would have it, I was in my Destiny disguise. But if I hadn't had the protection of pretending to be someone else, I might not have had the guts to tell him about my sister Dawn. You probably all remember that my younger sister has a great singing voice and has been trying for years to get her big break. Well, as Destiny, I had the nerve to tell this agent about her. He was interested enough for me to arrange a meeting for the three of us. I couldn't very well meet him again as my real self. He would probably think I was some kind of a nut! So I had to set up his meeting with Dawn on my next Destiny night. That meant I had to tell Dawn about Destiny. But she is sworn to secrecy, also.

"I want you all to know that something good did come out of the Destiny Club. The agent was impressed and signed Dawn as a client. He is in the process of negotiating a recording contract for her. Because of him, she has been hired as the opening act for the headliner of a show that opens next month at one of the larger neighborhood casinos. In fact, the three of us got together to celebrate during my last time as Destiny. I'm sure it never would have happened without Destiny's help. Being Destiny gave me the extra courage I needed."

I felt my face flush in embarrassment. *How could I have thought that Tiffani and Dawn would be involved in a ménage a trois? I simply had to learn to rein in my imagination!*

Nikki started laughing. "Well, since everyone else is confessing their 'sins,' tell them what happened the other night when you were Destiny, Julie."

"Geez, what a close call that was!" admitted Julie. "Since Nikki's husband was out of town on business, Nikki and I had arranged to have dinner together at Portofino in the Mirage on my Destiny night . . . you know, that really posh, expensive restaurant? And while we were there we ran into a guy Nikki used to work with when she lived in California. Well, he was feeling pretty good, recently divorced, and had some extra comp tickets to the Cirque Beatles show, *Love*. He insisted we join him, refusing to take 'no' for an answer. So we ended up accompanying him to *Love*, and I have to say we really enjoyed ourselves."

"Tell him the rest of it, Julie." Nikki prompted.

Julie blushed, as she said: "That's all."

"No, that's not all," said Nikki. "He was hitting on Julie like crazy! We tried to politely ditch him after the show, but were unsuccessful. He even tried following us back to the apartment. We had to stop at an all-night coffee shop to wait until he finally got tired and left us alone before Julie could return to the apartment to change and go home. The way he was coming on to her we surely didn't want him to know the location of the apartment."

Throughout Nikki's narration, Julie continued to blush, and she mumbled something about it being Destiny he was really lusting after, not her.

I was blushing, too, which no one noticed . . . or if they did notice, they just thought I was flushed from the wine. But again, I was embarrassed at also suspecting Julie and Nikki of being into three-somes; and worse, of considering them capable of being a serial killer duo.

"Well, I also have an admission to add," said Amber. "As you all might remember, I was an avid swimmer in high school. And since I've been back in Las Vegas, I've taken it up again, working at it every day in my pool, weather permitting. One evening when Deena was Destiny, she met one of the producers of *O*, you know, the Cirque water show at the Bellagio. She began telling him about me, and he wanted to meet me. She set up a meeting, and of course it had to be again on one of her Destiny nights since that was the way he knew her. First we went to see the show, and then afterwards we got to stay and go backstage to meet some of the performers. And, well, he wanted me to audition for the show! I did, and he offered me a job! Can you believe it? It would be for only a small group part. But can you believe I could really be in *O*? I'm still debating on whether or not I'll do it. I'm afraid it would be too demanding of both my time and my energy. But I am unbelievably honored that I have the chance. That's the important thing, knowing that I *can* do it if I want! "

Everyone started talking at once, with most of us encouraging Amber to give it a shot. She had been a fabulous swimmer in high school—almost part fish.

"Okay," she agreed, "I'll give it some more thought before making my decision. But that's not the end of my news. I was so grateful to Deena that I wanted to pay her back in kind. You remember she did some modeling shortly after we all graduated, and she still has those long, great legs of a twenty-year-old. I asked my source at *O* if he had any connections with modeling agents because I had a friend who would be perfect . . . of course he didn't know it was Deena because he only knew her as Destiny. He set up a meeting with a modeling agent, only this time I was Destiny and Deena was herself. Since Larry was out of town on business, I had already planned to have dinner with Kayla, anyway, so we invited her to come along for luck.

The agent was so impressed with Deena that he has agreed to represent her in doing photography modeling—particularly leg modeling . . . stockings, ankle and toe jewelry—things like that. And while we were at our meeting, we got to talking about children and grandchildren—you all know how adorable Kayla's granddaughters are. Well, she showed him some pictures of them, and he *also* wants to represent her granddaughters for modeling! We all met again to celebrate at The Chandelier Bar and then had dinner at Scarpetta. So Destiny ended up being good to the three of *us*, as well as to Tiffani and Dawn."

Throughout the confessions of the others I kept watching Nikki. But she just smiled and never let on about the secret fantasy she had been acting out. As I had promised myself earlier, I allowed her secret to remain private, even though I practically had to bite my tongue to keep from telling everyone. I was disappointed that she hadn't decided to share her experience with us, and I hoped she would be able to continue with it without the protection of her Destiny façade. If she did, perhaps someday she would reveal that part of her life to us and even invite us to come along to share in the enjoyment of her musical talent. I guess I could relate somewhat to her, because I had never shared my pole dancing lessons with anyone, either.

"What about you, Jayne?" asked Kayla. "You never shared much of what you did on your Destiny nights, other than doing things you could do without the added courage of the Destiny disguise. Do you have anything exciting to tell us? We know you can never replace Marc in your heart; but have you met anyone yet that you could at least feel comfortable going to a movie with, or out to dinner with?"

I could feel myself blushing. When it came right down to it, I was no different than Nikki in keeping secrets from the others. I almost told them. I came so close to divulging my secret pole dancing classes that the words were on the tip of my tongue. But instead, I shook my head and took a gulp of wine. "Nope, nothing exciting," I said, feeling a little guilty; I just didn't feel like I was ready yet to tell them, or anyone else about it, yet. But maybe soon . . . maybe after all of the Destiny mess that I had created was cleared up.

It seemed that Destiny *had* been beneficial to some of us—beneficial to some of us more than others. . . . But even that would never be able to make up for the murders. I still felt a bit foolish that I had even remotely considered any of my friends could be into kinky sex and/or serial killing.

After we enjoyed some good laughs about our Destiny experiences, the conversation turned serious. I felt bad having to put a damper on our celebration, but they needed to know what I had learned. I related the details of my tidying up the apartment in trying to get rid of any evidence of ourselves ever having been there. They all looked stunned and started talking at once. They couldn't believe that none of them had thought of clearing out the apartment. "Why didn't you call us to help you, Jayne," asked Julie, her question quickly echoed by the others.

"I didn't feel like I could take the time. The apartment was the official address for the woman known as Destiny Aaron. Therefore, it seemed obvious that when Metro finds no connection between the alleged serial killer and the apartment, they will be back to question us some more; there are just too many unanswered details pertaining to us. That is why I felt an overwhelming urgency last night that the apartment needed to be done at once; so I just did it. I hope I was able to get rid of all traces of us, because this morning I drove by and there was a Crime Scene Investigation unit parked in front of the building. So don't forget. We need to be on guard. We are still nowhere near being in the clear."

Thankfully, at least for us anyway, the mystery was solved of how Chloe and Destiny were connected to the serial killer. So that was one thing we no longer had to worry about. We passed around the newspaper article with the serial killer's photo, each of us giving it a careful study. The scary part was, in his photo without his Destiny disguise, he was an attractive, normal-looking man. We could all see how Chloe had been attracted to him. Any of us could have been. It just goes to show you can never tell what people are really like by their looks alone.

We ended our evening together by making a solemn pact that if the police continued to question us about our part in the capture—or anything else related to Destiny—we would deny any knowledge. We would stick to our story that we had merely been trying to be good citizens and had just gotten lucky. I didn't tell the others that I was still worried about explaining how Destiny's Social Security number could be the same as my deceased grandmother's. I would just have to keep insisting that it was merely some kind of an unexplainable fluke.

The only memento left from our Destiny escapade was the wig, which Chloe still had. I told her I would dispose of it for her; but she said it was something she needed to take care of herself. She said she had almost burned it in the fire pit in her backyard this morning, but then decided it might benefit someone . . . perhaps a cancer survivor who had lost her hair while undergoing chemotherapy. The wig could always be restyled. She said that as soon as she felt up to it she would contact the American Cancer Society.

A few days later we each received a telephone request from Detective Samson for another meeting at Metro to go over our statements again. Even though in the back of my mind I had been halfway expecting his call, when it actually happened I was momentarily numb. Although his request was framed in the form of a voluntary meeting, we viewed it as being a mandatory summons; we all felt we had no choice in not complying. We settled on a time and date when we were all available to go together. I felt a tingle of excitement at the thought of possibly seeing Lieutenant Norman again, hoping that I would; but I also wondered just what that hoping meant? *Was I actually becoming attracted to him? Or was it a weird kind of something else that I was feeling?* Again, I had been out of the game too long to trust what I was feeling, or to even know if I *was* feeling something.

When we arrived at the station, instead of being taken into an interrogation room like where we had been questioned on the night we had captured the serial killer, we were escorted into what looked more like a conference room. Rather than Detective Samson, it was Lieutenant Norman who was seated at the head of a large table. Strangely, even as nervous as I was, I couldn't help noticing that he was nicely dressed in grey trousers, a darker grey long sleeved shirt, and a grey and maroon striped tie. I also noted again what an attractive man he was. *How could I be thinking this? Was I nuts?*

He smiled hospitably as he said, "Good afternoon, ladies. How nice to see you all again. The reason I requested you all here is to ask you to go over once more exactly what occurred on the night you captured the serial killer; I want to see if anything has jogged your memories that might result in new information."

He proceeded to go over our story again, trying to prod for more details, which made me think he was probably hoping to trip us up in some way. He kept glancing at me, specifically, even while interviewing the others.

We doggedly persisted in sticking to our story of accidentally having been in the right place at the right time. Finally he stopped, apparently realizing that further questioning would yield nothing productive. Then he changed tactics, perhaps in hope of riling us into admitting something, and revealed what Metro had learned: the alleged killer had confessed to becoming so obsessed with a glamorous woman named Destiny Aaron that he couldn't tolerate her being with other men. He began stalking her, then dressing as her to lure to their deaths the men she had been with earlier on the given nights. He was thirty-nine years old and resided in North Las Vegas, where he had his own tax-accounting/investment business. He had never been married, and even though he had been picked up and questioned several times in the past for allegedly stalking women, there had never been enough evidence to indict him.

Lieutenant Norman finished his dialogue with a statement that startled all of us: "So you see, ladies, we still have a very large loose end to tie up. There is still a woman out there, somewhere, named Destiny Aaron, who also fits the description of the person of interest we have been looking for. . . ."

He eyes slowly moved over us, one by one, making a point of searching each of our eyes. *Trying to assess our reactions*, I thought. As the seconds ticked by, I began to feel the betraying heat of guilt rising to my face. In an effort to hide it before his eyes reached me, I bent my head in an invented coughing fit.

He gave me a strange look. "Are you all right, Ms. Robbins?"

"Yes, sir. It's just my allergies," I answered, taking hefty swigs from the water bottle I carried in my purse.

"Well, thank you all for coming in," he said, rising to his feet. "If any of you remember something that you think may be helpful, even in the smallest way, please get in touch with me," he added, handing each of us his card.

On the way out, I couldn't help thinking: *Darn, the first man I meet since losing Marc that I find attractive has to be a homicide cop trying to find evidence that I'm some kind of a criminal! What kind of crummy luck is that?*

It was when we were in the parking lot heading to our cars that it suddenly hit me: he hadn't been assessing our reactions at all. He had been looking to see if any of us had dark blue violet eyes. "Oh, God," I cried! If any of you still have your Destiny contact lenses, flush them as soon as you get home!"

CHAPTER 23

—————— • • • ——————

A WEEK LATER I received another phone call from Metro, this time from Lieutenant Norman, himself. When I looked at the Caller ID, my first instinct was not to answer. But that would have only prolonged the inevitable. Even though in one way I very much wanted to see him again, in another way I *never* wanted to see him again.

"Hello," I managed to answer in a cheery tone that I hoped sounded blasé.

"Hello. This is Lieutenant Norman. May I please speak with Ms. Robbins?"

"This is she," I replied, hoping that my blaséness would suggest an innocent, carefree demeanor (one that I certainly didn't feel!).

"Ms. Robbins, before we can officially close the case, we still have a few more questions regarding you and your friends' help in capturing the alleged serial killer. Since you seem to be the spokesperson for the group, I would appreciate it if you would come down to the station again so we can talk about it in more detail?"

I noticed he had phrased it in the form of a question, rather than as a demand.

Had he found me out? I wondered. Again, my first instinct was to hedge; but I decided I really needed to get it over with. I hated having it hanging over my head. I knew all I could do was to continue to stick to the same story that I and the others had been giving him until he accepted, once and for all, that there was nothing more to it. I just hoped that when I did meet with him that this would be the last of the questioning.

"Yes, sir. When would you like for me to come?"

"Oh, say, in about thirty minutes? Would that work for you? I'm here now at the station."

"Yes, sir, I'll be there." My hands were shaking as I hung up the phone.

I had to concentrate carefully on my driving, which may have been a good thing, besides safety reasons: it kept my mind occupied so I couldn't dwell on my fear of what I might be facing. When I arrived, I informed the desk officer that I was there to see Lieutenant Norman per his request. This time, instead of being taken to an interrogation room or into the conference room like last time, I was escorted into a small, private office. It was sparsely furnished, with only a desk and desk chair, a large file cabinet, a bookshelf filled with books, and two chairs of the type typically found in the waiting rooms of doctors and dentists. However, Lieutenant Norman was nowhere in sight. I was given the offer to sit in one the chairs and asked to wait. I was grateful to be able to sit down, because my fear and dread had returned, and I was beginning to feel rubbery-legged. I crossed my ankles, folded my hands in my lap, and tried to relax. I was in the process of taking a few deep breaths when the door opened and Lieutenant Norman walked in.

My heart skipped a beat. He was looking as attractive as he had the last time I had seen him. And, again, he was dressed in greys: grey trousers, a shirt with small, subdued, grey and white stripes, and a dark grey tie. *Geez, I hoped he didn't fancy himself another Christian Grey.* I immediately felt my face reddening at the absurd thought, which made me even more uncomfortable.

He gave me a genial smile. "Thank you for coming so quickly, Ms. Robbins. I hope you will please excuse me for making you wait; right after I talked to you I had a minor emergency come up that required my immediate attention."

"No, that's quite all right," I said, returning his genial smile in my continuing attempt to convey a blasé demeanor. I hoped to give him the impression that I had nothing to be worried about.

"Would you like something to drink?" he asked cordially. "Water, coffee, a soft drink, perhaps?"

"No, thank you, I'm good," I answered, although my mouth was already beginning to feel dry from apprehension.

He studied me for several seconds before resuming. "You know, Ms. Robbins, one thing still bothers me about the serial killings. We have uncovered plenty of evidence which should certainly prove that the suspect we have in custody is indeed the serial killer who has been eluding us for months. In fact, he has already confessed and is working towards a plea of insanity. He's claiming that his obsessive jealousy of the woman known as Destiny Aaron is what compelled him to murder other men she was seeing—in essence, crimes of passion.

"We still believe that this woman, Destiny Aaron, could shed valuable light on the case and would be an important witness for the prosecution. Our problem is, she seems to have disappeared. We were able to trace her residence through her address with the DMV. However, even though she had a Nevada driver license, she apparently never owned a car. We traced the car she used to take her driving test to a used car lot in Henderson."

A chill ran through my body. *Had Rolf given him Julie's name . . . or worse, my name? Is that why Lieutenant Norman has summoned me here?* My ears began to ring and I felt light headed, like the blood was rushing from my brain. I feared I might pass out if I didn't put my head between my knees. But I couldn't do that. It would give me away! So instead, I deliberately let my purse slide from my lap onto the floor. When I bent down to pick it up, I took my time. Thankfully, after I straightened up again with my purse back on my lap, the lightheadedness was somewhat better. I hoped Lieutenant Norman hadn't seen through my ruse. I forced myself to try to calm down and concentrate on what he was saying.

He was gazing at me, a slight frown making a furrow between his eyebrows. "Are you all right, Ms. Robbins? You look a little pale. Are you sure you wouldn't like some water?"

"No, no, I'm fine, just clumsy," I replied, making a poor attempt at a self-deprecating chuckle.

"Very well. Now let's see, where was I . . . oh, the owner of the car lot, Rolf Kelly, said a woman fitting Destiny Aaron's description arrived there with a friend. After looking around, the friend told Mr. Kelly she was interested in buying a certain car and wanted to take it for a test drive. He agreed, and apparently that was when the said friend drove the car to the DMV for Destiny Aaron to take her driving exam. We asked Mr. Kelly if he was in the habit of allowing just anyone to take one of his cars for a test drive without him along. He said he often did when he was at the lot alone and would make a copy of the person's license as a safety precaution. He had done so in this case, and that's when we finally thought we had a clue to finding out Destiny Aaron's true identity—through her friend. But Mr. Kelly said when the car was returned, the woman had decided she didn't want to buy the car after all. Therefore, since he had no further reason to keep the copy of her license, unfortunately for us, he had thrown it away.

"The apartment in Destiny Aaron's name has been vacated, and the bank account in her name has been closed, along with all of the utilities. Even stranger, when we went over Destiny Aaron's apartment, it had been wiped clean of fingerprints, and there were no personal items left behind . . . except for one."

I felt my pulse quicken, and the beginning of the lightheadedness again.

"Yes," he continued, "shoved way under the bed we found a hair brush. After it had gone through forensics we learned it is the kind of hair brush used primarily for wigs. There were even a few strands of red hair in the brush, which analysis showed to be synthetic, probably from a wig. The brush also had some fingerprints on it. . . ." His voice trailed off, as if he were waiting for me to say something.

My heart began to hammer inside my chest. *Damn! That was the one place I had forgotten to check with my hurried cleanup: under the bed!* I just looked at him, so stunned by his news that I was temporarily speechless! I prayed that my eyes wouldn't give me away by showing the fear that I felt.

"Unfortunately, we were unable to match the fingerprints to any we have on file, including the suspect's. It's strange. Like I said before, it's as if Destiny Aaron has just disappeared—almost as if she never really existed. We still have a warrant out for her as a possible material witness, but we don't have much hope of finding her. So you see—if there is anything you can remember that might help, anything at all. . . ." He sighed deeply and shrugged his shoulders.

I, of course, was nearly giddy with relief! Thank God I hadn't accepted Lieutenant Norman's offer of something to drink! He hadn't made the offer out of hospitality, I now realized. It had been a ploy in hopes of obtaining my fingerprints! I was sure of it! The fingerprints found on the hairbrush could belong to any of us, including me! It was sheer dumb luck that I hadn't taken him up on his offer! I experienced an inner "whew," and my heartbeat began a more regular rhythm as I fought to maintain control. However I was careful not to show it, and I tried to look empathetic. "Well, I'm sorry, but I really don't see how I can help you." I said. I was more than ready to leave, and I started to rise from my chair.

He held up his hand. "A few more minutes, please. Indulge me. I haven't gotten to the specific reason why I thought you, in particular, besides being the spokesperson for your friends, might be the one who would able to help. As I'm sure you will recall, the social security number used on the bank account in Destiny Aaron's name belonged to your late grandmother. Now, are you absolutely sure that you haven't remembered any possible kind of connection that Destiny Aaron might have had with your grandmother?"

I was proud of myself that I was able to give him my blasé smile again, look him in the eye, and with crossed fingers behind my back state innocently: "No, sir, I cannot think of any possible contact my late grandmother might have had with Destiny Aaron."

He sighed again, and continued to hold my gaze. "Well, Miss Robbins, if you do happen to think of anything that might help us, you won't hesitate to contact me?" He rose to his feet. "Here is another one of my cards, in case you misplaced the others I've given you."

I continued to sit as I took the card he offered. He watched as I made a small production of opening my purse and tucking his card safely inside. It was my way of stalling for time to get my thoughts together. I couldn't help feeling him giving me his card again was his way of letting me know that he knew that I knew more than I was telling him. But I also knew that he knew that he would likely never be able to find out what I knew. Finally he looked away.

I was still shaken at how easily I could have incriminated myself by accepting one of his proffered drinks so that he could obtain my fingerprints. My heart was still beating much faster than normal.

"Again, I thank you for coming in, Ms. Robbins."

I couldn't stall any longer, and I fervently hoped that my legs wouldn't shake as I rose to leave. I was almost to the door when he said, "Ms. Robbins, I see that you're a widow?"

Surprised, I stopped and turned back to face him. "Yes, sir, I am."

His voice softened. "I'm very sorry for your loss." He hesitated a few seconds. "Maybe our paths will cross again sometime, socially. And, by the way, if they do, please don't call me sir. It makes me feel old. My name is Andy," he added with an unexpected grin.

I nodded and gave him a half smile before turning to make a hasty retreat. My emotions were such a bewildering mixture that I felt I had to get out of there . . . fast!

After that meeting, we received no further "requests" from Metro for additional questioning. I guess they had to accept the reality that none of us were ever going to give them any additional information. Eventually, we were notified that the case had been officially closed and that the serial killer suspect was incarcerated and awaiting trial. To our advantage, in subsequent news statements, Metro skimmed over our part in the apprehension of the fugitive, wanting to give themselves the major share of credit. None of us were ever subpoenaed as witnesses, and none of our names were ever mentioned in the news. The only time our pictures had appeared on TV was on that very first broadcast Chloe had seen—which she insisted wasn't clear enough for any of us to have been easily recognized. The married ones in the group were even able to conceal the whole Destiny affair from their husbands, other than Kayla, of course. Most importantly, Metro has never been able to find the mysterious, ever-elusive woman named Destiny Aaron.

CHAPTER 24

———— • • • ————

SEVERAL MONTHS LATER, Julie and I paid a visit to Fremont Street, treating ourselves to a lush dinner at Oscar's, the posh, old-Vegas-style restaurant owned by our former mayor of many years, Oscar Goodman. Even though it was a chilly evening, we strolled along the Fremont Street Experience, under the canopy, stopping to enjoy the laser show. When we resumed our walk, I saw a woman in a Snow White costume. However, on closer inspection, even though her costume was similar, she was not the same woman I had talked with when I was trying to obtain Destiny's fake driver license. Out of curiosity, I stopped and asked her if she knew what had happened to the previous Snow White. And, to my delight, she said that the former Snow White had gotten a job with a major movie studio as a costume designer and had moved to California with her daughter.

I was also curious to see if Jade was still performing, and when I saw the large crowd gathered around what I considered to be "her place," I was certain that she was. As Julie and I moved closer, I could hear her music. We paused to take a quick peek, and when I saw that Jade was in mid performance of her sword dance, we stayed long enough for Julie to see it to the end. By the way Julie's eyes widened, I could tell she was as enraptured with Jade as I had been. I didn't want to take the off chance of Jade remembering me, so as she was completing her last spin, Julie and I hurried away to reward ourselves with a drink. I made sure it was not one of the establishments where I had treated Snow White or Jade to drinks when I was trolling for Destiny's driver license.

Julie ordered her usual cabernet, and I, on a whim, ordered a raki, which actually turned out to be pretty good in an unusual sort of way. Stopping for drinks gave us a pause to reflect, and we sat quietly for several moments with neither of us speaking. As we each became lost in our own thoughts, I was reminded of my curiosity about Julie's relationship—for lack of a better word—with Rolf. The only way I would know would be to just come right out and ask her.

"Julie, we have been friends for a very long time, and I hope I'm not being too presumptuous in asking . . . but just what is your relationship with Rolf? I've never heard you mention him.

Julie gave me an exaggerated, mysterious smile and raised her eyebrows. "I don't know if I should tell you or keep you in suspense," she said, giving a mockingly wicked chuckle. Then she took hold of my hand and changed to a serious tone.

"Well, Jayne, it's rather a long story. While all of you were off pursuing your fortunes, you remember I remained in Vegas. I was going through a rocky period in my first marriage, and to fill some of my time I began volunteering as a counselor at a shelter for abused women. One of the women was Rolf's sister. She had been in a severely abusive relationship, both physically and emotionally. Although her boyfriend had beaten her numerous times in the past, he finally injured her so severely that she ended up in the hospital. As it so often happens with abused women, she was planning to return to live with him after she was well enough to be released. He had pleaded with her to come back with him, vowing he would never hurt her again. And she believed him, even though he had made that same promise each time he had beaten her in the past.

"Rolf intervened, and convinced her to come live at the shelter, instead. During my counseling sessions with her, she found enough inner strength to be able to cut ties with her abusive boyfriend and start a new life without him.

"Unfortunately, in the beginning she went through a few scary times when her boyfriend threatened and stalked her; but she was able to retain her strength and resolve and had him placed under a restraining order. That was when he finally gave up and hooked up with a new girlfriend to abuse. Only his new girlfriend wasn't as lucky. He ended up killing her and is now in prison. Rolf believed that I had saved his sister's life. He felt so indebted to me that he told me if he could ever do anything for me—anything, other than committing murder—for me to just ask. So that is how we ended up with the car in which you were able to take Destiny's driving test. And he's not bad in the sack, either!"

Her last statement left me speechless, with my mouth literally flying open. Julie started laughing so hard her eyes began to water! "You should see your face!" she guffawed. "I'm kidding! I'm kidding, she said as she began to dry her eyes. Sorry, I just couldn't resist. I thought we both could use a little humor . . . but, seriously, I think Rolf did have a crush on me."

I was still trying to get over the initial shock of her revelation, even though she insisted she had been joking. Somewhere in the back of my mind a little part of me couldn't help wondering if perhaps it could be true . . . Rolf was attractive in a blatantly sexy sort of way. Then I reminded myself of my ridiculous suspicions about my friends while I was doing my sleuthing. I smiled and nodded as I said, "Good one, Julie. You really got me."

Then, I almost told her about my pole dancing; however the quiet, intimate mood of sharing had been shattered with her kidding remark about Rolf. But I knew that someday—someday soon—I would tell her about it.

I'm glad Julie and I paid our visit to Fremont Street when we did, before it changed. I'm especially glad we happened along at the right time for her to get to see Jade. Since our visit, a new ordinance was passed affecting Fremont Street artists. Under the new ordinance, they are only allowed to perform for two hours at a time in one specific area. I wondered how the ordinance was affecting Jade? Somehow, I was sure that she had been able to find a way around it, or perhaps had even moved to a higher-end venue away from Fremont Street. She was certainly talented enough, and she was shrewd enough, too. It was obvious that Jade was a survivor! But for sure, with the new ordinance, Fremont Street would never be the same, I reflected. In an odd way, it made me sad. It also made me wonder if I would have been able to make the connection to obtain Destiny's driver license if the new ordinance had already been in place.

Although the Destiny Club is now officially history, we still meet weekly for our luncheons. Looking back, we agreed that we all did really enjoy—albeit each in her own unique way—creating an alternate identity to dress up as and engage in role playing. Therefore, if any one of us should decide at some time in the future to again pursue a double life, it would be up to her to personally devise her own identity and disguise. Whether or not she would want to share any of that information with the rest of us, well, that would be strictly her decision. Right now, we're all still pretty somber as we continue the recovery process from the results of our folly. I do hope that someday we will be able to recapture some of our whimsy that we enjoyed during the reign of the Destiny Club.

Another good thing to come out of the Destiny Club is that we are closer to one another now than we have ever been. At present, we're helping each other learn to work through our guilt, as well as gradually finding acceptance that we were not to blame for some crazy person becoming obsessed with one of us and committing murders. It could have happened without the Destiny Club. It could conceivably have happened to some other woman—any other woman, rather than to Chloe. The universe is full of random happenings, often seemingly without reason.

We have all decided to take a cruise together in six months or so, without any husbands along. We feel that the luxurious, care-free ambiance afforded by a cruise will aid in ridding our guilt; that perhaps getting away will help to put things back into proper perspective. I thought one of those mystery cruises might be fun. One of those cruises where a pretend murder is committed aboard ship for the passengers to solve. It would be a safe fictitious murder this time, where none of us would be personally involved.

As for me, I learned that if I had been taking a "Sleuthing 101" course, I would have flunked. I'll never have the detective skills of a Kinsey Millhone, a Nero Wolfe, or a Hercule Poirot. Not even close. I could also never be a legitimate private investigator; I would never be able to endure the long, boring stakeouts. Although I'm still learning to cope with the acceptance that I will have to go on with my life without Marc, for the most part I think I'm doing much better. Even though I continue to often feel his presence giving me strength—and I hope I always will—once in a while there are days that can still be excruciatingly painful. Sometimes just the smallest, unexpected thing— a smell, a sound, etc., will spark such a poignant, bittersweet memory that I descend into a temporary downward spiral. But I have also realized that the part of me capable of being attracted to another man is not dead. That someday I might even be able to find love again. As part of my healing process in dealing with my life change, I have been writing a novel about our adventure—fictionalizing the story and changing our names to protect our identities. Hally is my devoted co-writer, usually napping on my lap as I sit at my computer. I find the writing cathartic, and I think Marc would be happy that I am finding a positive way to try to fill some of the void in my life.

I had an unexpectedly pleasant surprise yesterday: Lieutenant Norman called and said he would like to meet me for coffee sometime— purely social. Instead of using his title, he even used his given name of Andy. I told him I would like that, and we arranged to meet next week.

Seriously, I think deep down he believes that I am the elusive Destiny Aaron. I can't help but smile whenever I think that if my novel is ever published, what he would think if he read it. And who knows? This just might be *the* story—the story that will prove to be my big break into being a successful author! This may sound trite, but I still like to think that if we believe in our dreams and follow our passions, we never know what wonders could be lying in store for us just around the bend. . . .

Epilogue

WELL, SINCE YOU'RE reading this, obviously it *was* published. Although some of you may be wondering if this novel is purely fiction, or, if in fact, it really did happen, there is no way you can ever know for sure. Some of you, especially some of you who happen to live in Las Vegas, may even imagine that you know who we are. However, being that when the serial killer was arrested none of us were ever referred to in the media by name—or in any other way; and since we all pledged a vow of secrecy never to reveal anything about the Destiny Club in the future, I will have to plead the fifth. I am afraid the answer to that question must forever remain a mystery. As the saying goes: "What happens in Vegas stays in Vegas!"

Previous Books by M.J. Walton

The Mizpah Coin

The Stories In Her Eyes
(Published under M.J. Pennington)

46496360R00117

Made in the USA
Middletown, DE
02 August 2017